Lighter Shade of Brown

Vicki Andrews

INDIGO

Indigo is an imprint of
Genesis Press, Inc.
315 Third Avenue North
Columbus, Mississippi 39701

ISBN 1-885478-75-5

Manufactured in the United States of America

FIRST EDITION

Acknowledgements

I cannot say enough about my editor, Karla Hocker—without her guidance and superb insight, this story would not be as good as it is. Thank you.

Without my family supporting me, urging and encouraging me, it would be impossible to accomplish something like this. To my son and daughter, all my love pours through these pages to both of you—I want you to be proud of me, too. And to my sister-friends, women I will love with all my heart, all my life, thanks for putting up with me, for guiding and helping me find...me.

Lighter Shade of Brown

Chapter 1

Chewing at the minuscule snatch of nail on one hand, clutching the steering wheel with the other, Danithia Gilberts peered intently at each street sign. She wondered where exactly she was. The glare from the intense Colorado sun temporarily blinded her, as did the beautiful array of fall colors. The golden leaves of the turning aspen trees were striking, but Danithia paid little attention to that. Her mind was rapidly shifting from scanning street signs to recalling the reason she was on this road, trying to find her way to a potential client. Lawyers don't usually make house calls, and, frankly, Danithia had never made one. But here she was going out of her way, driving through ritzy neighborhoods looking for the historical mansion which housed Ms. Griffin, an extremely wealthy elderly woman, someone she'd met only briefly about a year ago. Danithia knew very little about her, except that she was a very successful author of ethnic romantic fiction. But neither the wealth nor the occupation were the reasons Danithia was coming to see her. In fact, she wasn't particularly interested in representing a writer, but it was the haunting tone of the woman's voice—the pleading actually—that put her on this road today.

Danithia spotted the First Avenue sign, flicked the left blinker, and headed toward Cherry Creek and the home of Ms. Patricia Griffin.

~ ~ ~

The private road she was looking for said "Griffin Way," and it was discreetly tucked away. The road wound its way up to a mansion that, in all its glory, resembled a castle. Danithia's breath caught as her eyes took in its architectural splendor. A guttural moan of appreciation escaped her, and deep inside she wished for this kind of wealth. She gazed at the impressive structure, and her mind conjured up visions of times gone by when damsels in distress leaned from towers like these, searching for a knight to rescue them.

The mansion was obviously 19th century, but it managed to maintain an air of elegance. A cool breeze gently caressed her face at the exact moment when she imagined she could feel the spirits of those who had built it hundreds of years ago. Probably slaves who had migrated west in search of freedom, only to find themselves laboring long and hard to erect this magnificent structure. One they would never live in. One they would never enjoy.

She pressed the doorbell and waited, attempting to ready herself for whatever she was about to face. A sudden swish of forced air drew her gaze to the massive oak door as it opened. An elderly woman with a quick smile and warm, friendly demeanor welcomed her. Danithia judged her to be about sixty years old. She had wrinkled brown skin, an ample behind and bosom that made Danithia think of her granny. How warm and wonderful hugs from her granny always were, and how easy it was to get lost in the soft warmth of her bosom while listening to her tell her stories. She always smelled like home to Danithia. And instantly Danithia liked this stranger who seemed to chatter endlessly.

"The missus don't hardly receive no comp'ny any mo'. It sho is nice to see you here. Peoples call me Geraldine. I'm the missus housekeeper."

"Nice to meet you. I'm Danithia—Danithia Gilberts."

"And such a pretty gal, too. You married?"

"No ma'am. Haven't found the time . . . or the right man yet."

"Well don't you worry none 'bout that. A woman like you will get hitched soon enough." She patted Danithia's hand, as if to reassure her. "Yes indeed, it'll happen soon enough."

Danithia usually hated anyone patronizing her in this manner, but she smiled at her, knowing she meant well, she meant no harm or disrespect to Danithia or her choices.

"I'm not exactly craving the 'golden ring fantasy,' as my girlfriends call it, right now."

"Gettin' married ain't no fantasy! At times, it might be cold and harsh—challengin'—but I 'spect you know all about challenges. Marriage is just about the most beautiful thing you'll ever 'perience in this life." She paused. "'Cept for maybe bearin' a child. Nuttin' more wonderful than that neither!" She looked around the room as if she'd misplaced something. Danithia could tell she was lost in her thoughts.

They were still standing in the foyer, and Danithia took this moment of silence to admire it. The foyer was as beautiful as any she'd ever seen on television, with high ceilings and an expansive chandelier that twinkled, giving off a prism of colors as the sunlight hit it just right. This rainbow of light reflected beautifully on a round oak table which displayed a huge assortment of fresh flowers. It had pieces of kente cloth woven through the arrangement, giving it an ethnic flair. A beautiful tribute to mother Africa.

"Well now, listen to ole Geraldine, carryin' on like there's nuttin' better to do." She chuckled. "Let me go tell the missus you here. Would you like sumpin' to drink? You thirsty?" she asked, the question hanging like a high note in the air.

"If it's not any trouble, I'd love something cold."

"Iced tea? That okay?"

"That's fine. Thank you."

"You wait in here," Geraldine said as she led the way into a library. "I'll be right back."

She disappeared, leaving a lingering, pleasant scent of flowery perfume behind. When the door had closed, Danithia eagerly began to admire the portraits lining the south walls. She guessed they were pictures of Ms. Griffin's family. Black faces of men and women from long ago smiled at the camera, leaving a legacy of who they were for all to see. The men, she noticed, did not smile, instead they wore stoic expressions, while the women's smiles were broad and inviting. The clothing was dated: ruffled blouses, long skirts, huge feathered hats and tight lace-up boots, which, Danithia thought, must have killed their feet. In only two portraits were there any children in a more contemporary setting. Danithia guessed that the little girl was Ms. Griffin, and the little boy was perhaps her brother.

She circled the room, admired all the photographs, and still Ms. Griffin had not appeared. Neither had the iced tea. She smiled to herself, thinking the old woman probably forgot all about it. That's okay, she thought, I'm not all that thirsty anyway. But as five minutes of waiting turned into twenty, Danithia became impatient. She glanced at her watch for what seemed like the hundredth time and wondered what was taking Ms. Griffin so long. She sat in one of the flowered wing-back chairs and closed her eyes, trying to calm her impatient spirit.

"Here you go."

Danithia started, quickly opened her eyes, and sat erect.

"I'm sorry. Did I scare you? Takin' a little nap?"

"Not really. I was just resting my eyes for a moment. When will Ms. Griffin be here?"

"Oh." The elderly woman paused, looking sheepish. "It takes her a few minutes to get ready. She'll be along shortly. You help yoself to the 'freshments."

She left a silver tray with golden handles loaded with finger sandwiches and petite cookies for Danithia to enjoy. Two tall glasses of amber-colored tea with lemon were also there. Suddenly Danithia's thirst came back. She stirred in an artificial sweetener, and sipped the iced mixture. It was deliciously refreshing.

Nibbling a sandwich, she once again roamed around the room, stopping to read the spines of the numerous books that lined the northern wall. She chuckled at the titles, all indicative of romance novels: *Love Eternal, Sincerely Yours, To Hell and Back.* You got that right, Danithia thought as she read the last one. She didn't read romances. They never seemed to bear any resemblance to her own romantic experiences. She found it incredible, almost unbelievable, that this genre could gain someone the kind of wealth she was seeing reflected in this house, in Ms. Griffin's lifestyle. Danithia shook her head in disbelief, then thought maybe she should write a romance novel, then perhaps she, too, could be successful at writing about fantasy and fulfill her dream of being comfortably wealthy. Not a chance. She knew she was only creative when it came to writing a legal document, certainly not a steamy, decadent romance.

The grandfather clock chimed, and Danithia was surprised to see that she had now been there for an hour and she had not even spoken to Ms. Griffin. I wonder if I should just leave, she thought. Before this train of thought could completely take hold, a beautiful indigo-blue spine of a book caught her attention. She hesitated for only a moment before she decided to take it down. Curiosity got the best of her and she began to read.

~ ~ ~

Silently, Patricia Griffin entered the room and began to appraise the woman she hoped would become her ally. She noticed that not much about Danithia had changed since she had first met her over a year ago. Her height, already rather tall for a woman, was enhanced by three-inch heels. That touch of femininity contrasted sharply with the no-nonsense personality she remembered. Patricia watched her as she read and was impressed with her regal air, her posture as erect as that of a trained model. She had short hair, cut in an Afro and for reasons only Patricia could understand, that made her happy.

Patricia said, "I'm sorry to have kept you waiting."

Closing the book, Danithia spun. Her eyes widened at the sight of the black-draped figure facing her. She had recognized the voice as Ms. Griffin's, though it was raspier than she remembered, but she did not recognize the lady herself. Could not recognize her, since she was swathed in flowing black cloth from head to toe. Even her face was concealed beneath that black shroud of crepe-like material, and her hands were covered in black gloves.

The black garment had narrow slits in it for the eyes and the mouth. There was no slit for the nose and Danithia felt awkward staring at the face that was not a face. She tried to remain calm and professional, but her eyes darted around as she desperately sought somewhere else to look.

"Please," Patricia admonished, the black cloth fluttering, "don't be frightened."

"Ms. Griffin?" Danithia said, her own voice trembling.

"Yes, it's me."

"What's going on? Why are you dressed that way?"

"It's a long story and one which I'm going to share with you, if you've got the time." "This," she gestured, waving her black-gloved hand from the top of her head to her toes, "is the reason I called you here today."

Ms. Griffin crossed the room and sat on the sofa. She gestured for Danithia to join her. Feeling awkward, wary, and afraid, Danithia approached the seat opposite this figure in black and gingerly sat, ready to take flight at the slightest movement that seemed in any way threatening to her.

"I realize I should have warned you," said Ms. Griffin. "But I was afraid you wouldn't come if I did."

"What happened to you?"

She sighed, and the black cloth fluttered gently. "Do you recall the first time you and I met?"

"Yes. It was at the campaign dinner for Senator Brown. My firm sponsored that event. What does that have to do with this? Did you have an accident that night, or something?"

"An accident, oh God, how I wish this were all just an accident." Ms. Griffin paused. "Let me rephrase my question. Do you remember how we met?"

"You bumped into me. We almost had a red-wine disaster on my white cashmere suit." Danithia chuckled lightly as she remembered the way they both shrieked and began to rapidly apologize to one another. That was when they began to talk. Danithia remembered that Patricia Griffin was a beautiful woman, with a deep-ebony complexion, sparkling eyes, and a warm smile. She remembered she had beautiful white teeth that contrasted nicely with the dark tones of her skin. As they talked, Danithia recalled how very articulate, funny, and friendly she was.

Ms. Griffin said, "Later that same evening I also bumped into someone else. But before I tell you about

that, let me back up a bit." She paused as her eyes scanned
the room. She lifted a hand and pointed to the wall of family portraits.

"As you can see from the photographs in this room, I
am very proud of my family. I know who I am, where I
came from. I have a very rich heritage." She allowed her
hand to settle back on her lap, and again she took a deep
breath, causing the unnerving fluttering of the garment
again.

Danithia waited.

"I have always portrayed myself as a very proud
woman. From the time I was little, like in that photograph
there, it was drilled into me to be proud, stand up straight,
smile." She shook her head, then continued. "But along
with those admonitions came constant reminders that I was
black, blue-black in fact. And a gal as black as me had to
have something else to hold on to, because her looks
would get her nowhere. 'The blacker the berry, the sweet-
er the juice,' was a saying my classmates constantly taunted me with.

"So, I grew up thinking that I was never going to be
considered attractive by anyone because my skin was so
very, very dark. I tried to excel in every other area of my
life to hide the pain I felt looking at my face in a mirror.
My body was even darker than my face, and, deep inside,
I was not the proud Black woman I pretended to be.

"I never married. I didn't want to reveal my ugliness—
my body—to anyone if I didn't have to. So, I didn't."

Her voice turned wistful. "I began to write in a journal
when I was very young, and in it I revealed my innermost
fantasies. I could weave the most fanciful tales in my mind
and write them quite well on paper. It was then I discovered I could be a writer. All my main characters were

women . . . beautiful women . . . White women." She paused, giving Danithia a chance to absorb her words.

And Danithia did, feeling them deep inside herself, deep in the marrow of her bones.

"When I attended college," Ms. Griffin continued, "one of my professors in English literature found one of my essays particularly fascinating, and he convinced me to submit it for possible publication. With his help, I was able to successfully gain an agent, a publisher, editor, and, eventually, millions of dollars. But my fame and fortune never could completely erase my feelings of hatred for the darkness of my skin."

"But why?" Danithia asked, still unable to understand.

"Because, quite simply, I hated myself. I grew up in an era when White folks were horribly cruel, and you know what? So were the Blacks. Where did I fit in? In my mind, nowhere. So I escaped into a fantasy world of White beauty, love, and acceptance. And I hated myself even more for betraying my heritage."

"It must have been very hard for you."

"It was torture, and I must admit it was torture I put upon myself. Anyway, a cold reality was presented to me by my agent, who said I would never sell books about White characters since I'm Black. So he had someone edit my novels, rewrite my characters, giving them ethnic features and names. In essence, he made them Black. Eventually, as I matured as a writer and as a person, I began to conjure up images of beautiful Black people."

Danithia looked around the room, pointed to a portrait. "Conjure up images! You had so many beautiful examples within your midst."

"Yes I know, that's what makes this all the more troubling . . . I had a beautiful mother, grandmother . . . smart, strong women, but they didn't look like me. Do you understand what I'm saying?"

Danithia said nothing.

"Perhaps you don't. Over the years few people have," Ms. Griffin said sorrowfully. "Please don't hate me because you don't understand."

Danithia took a deep breath. "Ms. Griffin, I do not hate you. I'm just having a hard time understanding. That's all. I am not here to judge you."

"Eventually I began to accept myself. Well, at least I thought I had. At Senator Brown's fund-raiser I met—actually he bumped into me—a doctor. We began to chat and eventually he began to tell me about a new product—a patented formula—to lighten the skin. He said it was a revolutionary and exciting new product that he hoped the African American community would embrace. The more he talked, the more excited I got. When he told me it was very expensive, that was the least of my concerns. I have more than enough money to pay for practically anything I want. And . . . I wanted this. He told me they were looking for candidates for the first stage of human testing, and I jumped at the chance to be a . . . a . . . human guinea pig." She began to cry then, small whimpers and cat-like mews escaping her as the cape quivered and fluttered.

Danithia's heart went out to her. She whispered, "It didn't work, did it?"

"Well . . . yes," she hiccuped, "yes, at first it did work. After every treatment I saw my complexion lighten ever so slightly, and I was so pleased."

"I'm sorry, I don't understand. If it did work, why are you hiding yourself?"

"Six months into the treatment, I began to see blotches on my skin. They looked like tiny burns, kind of like a small blister. I first noticed them around my hairline, and this was shortly after I'd had my hair chemically relaxed."

Danithia gasped. "Did the two chemicals clash?"

"Initially, that's what I thought, but before I had a chance to either go back to my hairdresser or to Dr. Zimmerman, within days my entire face began exhibiting these blotchy, burn-like patches. I was covered with them." Her voice cracked. "I'm so ashamed, so very ashamed."

Danithia placed her arm around the other woman and allowed her to weep. Danithia could not see but imagined a cascade of uncontrollable tears falling down ebony cheeks, and it hurt her because she knew the pain Ms. Griffin must be feeling.

Ms. Griffin sniffed, "Have you ever heard the saying, 'be careful what you ask for?'"

"Of course I have . . . I'm sorry. So very, very sorry."

"I'll be all right," she said as she pulled away from Danithia's embrace. "More than anything what I want from you is not your sympathy, but your representation of me and anyone else who has gone through this skin-altering pigmentation process. But before we begin talking about that, I want you to see the monster I've become."

"All right," Danithia mumbled as she sat back, not sure she wanted to see what Ms. Griffin was talking about.

Ms. Griffin sighed heavily. She began to stand up, but it seemed as if it took a great deal of effort, as if her bones rebelled against each movement she made. She swayed slightly, then steadied herself. First, she began to remove the black gloves, pulling the material from each digit slowly. Her efforts finally resulted in the revelation of her left hand. It appeared to be mangled and contorted like that of a very old tree limb. The flesh was puckered, revealing an angry red tinge on each swollen, enlarged knuckle. There

were no fingernails. Danithia looked away as Ms. Griffin,
used her deformed left hand to finally remove the glove
from the right one. It too was in the same shape. Danithia
noticed the bony, raw flesh peeking through the sleeve at
her wrists, and she found herself repressing a shudder of
disgust.

Ms. Griffin again swayed slightly as she reached down
to gather the folds of the cloak in her fragile hands and, as
if in slow motion, she pulled the garment over her head.
With the unveiling finally complete, Danithia almost could
not believe her eyes. She did not see the once beautiful
face of Ms. Griffin that she had recalled earlier. Instead,
before her stood a woman whose face was hideously
scarred, marred like that of a burn victim. The skin left
revealed terribly injured tissue, red welts and abrasions
that traveled from her face and neck, down the entire
length of her arms.

The damage to her hands seemed so much worse
because not only were they burnt but they were also twisted in such a way that they appeared to have a deformity.
Danithia surmised that this was probably because the skin
on the hands is so much thinner, and the harsh chemical
had damaged her all the way to the bone.

Danithia's eyes traveled back up to Ms. Griffin's face.
Her mind was having a difficult time absorbing everything
she was seeing. To her complete and utter horror, in the
spot where a nose should have been, she saw only a hol-
low orifice. The bridge, nostrils, and contour of the nose
was virtually gone.

The gasp that escaped Danithia's lips was unintention-
al. The tears that fell from her eyes, the overwhelming sadness that gripped her at that moment surprised her. The
pain she saw reflected back in Ms. Griffin's eyes, held her.
She watched with fascination as one lone tear left a ragged

track of wetness as it slipped down a cheek that was rid-
dled with wrinkled, scarred skin.

She held out her arms, and the older woman fell into
them.

The two women held each other and each wept bitter
tears.

Chapter 2

everal hours later, once safely inside her car, Danithia grabbed her hand-held dictaphone and began to rapidly record the contents of her conversation with Ms. Griffin before the details escaped her memory. Although she had taken notes, she wanted more than anything to capture her feelings. The astonishing fact that Ms. Griffin knew there were other wealthy African Americans who had been treated by this Dr. Zimmerman. The idea that there could possibly be numerous other people disfigured, no doubt ashamed and banished from society, made Danithia feel literally nauseous.

As Danithia sat there and contemplated the enormity of the situation, she went from feeling righteously indignant to very sad. Today's events plunged her back in time to an incident that happened when she was in grade school. She didn't think she was any older than maybe seven or eight. A new girl had started coming to school shortly after moving into the neighborhood, and everybody loved to tease her. What was her name? Danithia couldn't immediately recall, then the name suddenly slammed into her head. . . Pam . . . and childhood memories about her flooded Danithia's head.

She remembered this little girl almost from the very first day she came to school. Her clothes were ragged but clean. She always had a thumb stuck in her mouth, and actually that turned out to be a good thing because, once she took it out, she had huge teeth, far too big for her mouth. Danithia remembered how crooked they were, there seemed to be too many of them and they were all clamoring for space, protruding and twisting at odd angles. She was a definite candidate for braces. The kids called her, among other things, Bucky Beaver. She also wore thick glasses that made her eyes look crossed, and she was real dark skinned. Danithia remembered how her friends would call her all kinds of names: black tar baby, jungle bunny, four eyes. They'd even chant, "Pam, Pam black not tan. She only eats Spam. Pam will chew a hole through you. If she could see, she'd eat you too!" And everybody would fall out laughing. But Danithia never did.

There was something about the girl that intrigued Danithia. She could identify it now, but her childhood immaturity didn't allow her to know what it was then. Pam had a distinctive air about her, a calm spirit. She was the type of person who would embrace you, accept you, and she would always keep your secrets. She was the kind of friend you'd want to have all your life.

Danithia remembered how hard Pam would try not to cry when people teased her mercilessly, but sometimes her lips would tremble and then, if she could get away, she'd run and hide until a teacher would look for her and drag her back to the classroom whimpering and wiping snot upon her sleeve. One day, it was particularly awful, and that was the day Danithia decided to try to befriend her. She waited for her after school, but the minute she'd called out her name and waved, Pam took off running, her long braids bouncing wildly behind her back.

"Wait!" Danithia screamed. "Wait, I just wanna walk home with you!"

But Pam just kept on running, it was as if she hadn't heard her. Danithia couldn't catch her even though she tried. Pam was used to running, running away from her tormentors. Danithia tried every day for a whole week.

Then she noticed that Pam didn't seem to be running quite as fast. She caught her and jogged beside her.

"Hi!"

No answer.

"Didn't your mama teach you it's rude not to speak?" Danithia said, taking a dangerous moment to stop and put her hand on her narrow hips, as if she were about to scold.

Pam stopped too, and her thumb came out of her mouth with an audible pop.

"Why you keep bothering me? You fixin' to call me names, too?"

"Heck no! I wanna be your friend."

Pam's eyes grew wide, enormously magnified by her thick glasses. "Why?" she asked.

"Cause."

"Cause what?"

"Cause you need one."

"No I don't," Pam said, sticking her thumb deep inside her mouth again.

"Uh huh, yes, you do," Danithia insisted.

They continued to walk in silence. Then Danithia said, "Can I see your glasses?"

"Why?"

"Just let me see 'em. I won't break 'em."

"Cross your heart!"

"And hope to die!" Danithia said while enthusiastically crossing the wrong side of her chest.

Pam handed them over, and Danithia put them on. Suddenly everything was distorted and grossly magnified. The sky looked close enough to touch. She remembered she even reached out to embrace the fluffy white clouds.

"Wow! This is cool."

"You crazy," Pam said, smiling.

Danithia turned awkwardly in a circle and was totally amazed at how much everything had changed the second she put those glasses on.

"Does stuff look like this to you, too?"

"No. My eyes is so bad, them glasses make everything look normal. Cause gurrrrl," Pam dragged, "I cain't hardly see!"

"Hold my hand," Danithia said excitedly, "can you guide me?"

"I just told you I cain't hardly see, how I'ma guide you when I cain't see . . . you're goofy."

"Come on," Danithia said, "let's try anyway."

And the two of them stumbled and laughed until tears streamed down their respective brown cheeks, neither one of them really able to see where they were going. They had so much fun that for weeks they'd meet after school, and Danithia would wear the glasses and they'd hold hands and tell each other all kinds of secrets. They became best friends for the next two years, until Pam moved away. The teasing stopped and other kids lined up to wear Pam's glasses after school. Danithia remembered how quick Pam was to forgive even her worst tormentors. Danithia didn't know it then, but she did now. Pam was a proud person. She was a wonderful human being and somehow Danithia knew that if she were to run into her today, Pam would be a beautiful woman.

Danithia smiled as she remembered her friend from so very long ago and wondered if her intense desire to help others stemmed from that brief childhood friendship with Pam. It probably did. What better way to help others than being a lawyer. It was a career to champion the cause of the underdog, the people society wants to abuse, misuse, and forget. Her five-year stint in criminal law left upon her an indelible print of man's inhumanity to man. Be it black, white, yellow, or brown, she had seen and heard it all: self-hatred, hatred of others, scorn for mothers, fathers, sisters, brothers, an absence of the essence—the meaning of love. Ms. Griffin wrote about fantastical, imaginary, practically non-existent romantic love, searching for an inkling of its likeness in her own life—her own loves. Fifty-nine years old, and she had not yet figured out the love she needed was inside herself. Even if she were pecan brown, caramel, high yellow . . . or even white . . . she'd still be unhappy.

Danithia sighed because now was not the time for her to reason why, her job was to find and exact justice for not only Ms. Griffin but all those caught in this web of deceit. This futile pursuit of happiness through lighter shades of brown.

~ ~ ~

Danithia rushed into her office and buzzed Patrick O'Leary's assistant asking her if he was available to speak with her. Fortunately, his calendar was clear the entire afternoon and Danithia was welcome to come to his office anytime. She was so happy that she didn't have to wait to reveal her potential case and pitch her idea for the firm handling this type of class action. Danithia grabbed her hand mirror, applied fresh lipstick, patted her hair in shape, and headed straight for Pat's office.

"Well, well. Look who's here. How's it going Danithia?" Pat asked, warmly welcoming her.

"Everything is going great, Pat. Thank you for seeing me on such short notice." She sat in the chair across from him and crossed her legs.

"Today is one of my rare slow days, so you're in luck. What can I do for you?"

She cleared her throat and tried to quiet the tremors she felt deep in her belly. She'd never done this before.

"I have a potential new case for the firm's consideration." She paused, taking a deep breath. "It's a bit unusual because though it's class action material, it does not
involve a securities fraud claim."

"Go on."

"Let me back up and start by telling you that I had the
most interesting meeting this morning with Ms. Patricia
Griffin. You may have heard of her. She's a writer."

"I have heard of her. In fact my ex-wife had one of her
books which I actually got a chance to read. Excellent
writer, excellent!" Pat said.

"Yes, she is. She has won numerous literary awards
and made many achievements in the book publishing business. Anyway . . . apparently she has recently been
involved in a clinical trial for a revolutionary skin lighten-
ing treatment that has gone terribly wrong."

"Wrong, as in—" Pat interrupted.

"She's disfigured . . . horribly burned. Her nose is . . .
well . . . it's virtually gone. She wears a black cloak to
hide herself." Danithia thought back on her initial reaction
upon first seeing Patricia. "Needless to say, this formula
backfired big time. It has left her, and no telling how many
others, with faces, necks, and hands that look burned, with
lots of scar tissue and severe skin damage."

Pat's brow wrinkled, "Do we know who manufactured
the product?"

"The only names I have right now are . . ." She glanced
at her notes. "A Dr. Zimmerman, who administered the
treatments, and a company called Comex Manufacturing,
out of Lakeside, Colorado. Ms. Griffin remembers seeing
that name on some of the bottles. She didn't have much
more information than that. I'll need to investigate further
who all the players are . . . from the manufacturer to the
inventors, et cetera."

"These treatments were performed in a doctor's office?"

"Yes, some sort of secluded clinic. It was this Dr. Zimmerman who approached Ms. Griffin about a year ago and pitched this product to her."

"He solicited her? That's incredibly nervy."

"It's more than nervy. It's criminal. He preyed on her, used her own self-esteem issues—her own weaknesses—against her."

"I've seen photographs of her. In my opinion, she's beautiful," Pat said.

"I agree, but her issue is with the depth of the pigment in her skin. She's very dark. She calls herself 'blue black,' a name she's often been taunted with." Danithia tapped a foot. "It amazes me that she was never able to see her own beauty."

"What's the scoop on Dr. Zimmerman, I mean is he trying to correct the problem?"

"He hasn't been seen in months. His once posh office is closed, the clinic deserted. He has dropped from the face of the earth—vanished."

"Very interesting. What's your angle?"

"Well, I'd like to get an investigator to try to dig up where this Dr. Zimmerman may have gone, if he somehow altered the product, or if it was sold as a lethal cream, designed to damage, or if it was all an accident. Ms. Griffin knows she and others were part of a clinical trial for the product. I'll have to see what I can find out about that. Also, I need someone to go to Comex Manufacturing, possibly shut them down while an investigation ensues."

"That's a Food and Drug Administration task. Have you notified them?"

"Not yet. I wanted to wait to speak with you to see if I have the firm's support and approval to pursue this action for the plaintiffs. I know it's not the kind of class action we

normally pursue, but—well—you should see her face!
Someone's going to sue the pants off Comex, and since Ms.
Griffin came to me first and asked that we represent her, I
think we should be the first to file a complaint on her
behalf, and any other victims, immediately. Ms. Griffin
thinks she knows of at least two others."

"What do you see as this firm's liability on a matter like
this?"

"Liability—I hadn't thought of it as a liability for the
firm. To the contrary, I see it as a means to explore the
humanitarian side of the law. A 'class action with heart' so
to speak. A case like this could change our reputation as
being sharks, always beating up on big businesses. We
have a legitimate claim for damages that is all too real and
highly visible."

"It does have a certain appeal. I'll ask Lyle to manage
and run it."

Danithia's face fell. She hadn't expected him to pass on
the role of managing partner in this matter.

"With all due respect, Pat, I'd like to control the case,
under your supervision, of course." Danithia paused,
expecting a reprimand for being so bold as to say she not
only wanted to run the case, but she also wanted to hand-
select the managing partner. This was dangerous behavior,
she knew, especially for an associate seeking partnership,
but her passion propelled her forward.

"Danithia, I'm not as young as I used to be, and my
caseload is heavy right now. I've got several matters going
to trial soon if they don't settle," Pat said, but noticing
Danithia's face, he added, "But let me think about it, and
I'll get back to you. Okay?"

"That's fine," Danithia said, but she wasn't through
making her pitch for him to back her. "Pat, it would be an
honor to work this case with you. I've learned so much

under your guidance over the years, and I trust you totally. And frankly, the sensitive nature of this case dictates a trusting situation.   These plaintiffs are vulnerable, afraid, severely damaged, and ashamed."

"Ashamed . . .?"

"Ashamed that they were suckered into a treatment to lighten their skin. Think about the implications!" She jumped from her chair and began pacing the room, her passion for Ms. Griffin's plight fueling her. "Their actions will be interpreted as attempting to be 'White,' and we're talking about wealthy, influential African Americans here. They can't lose face in their own community! We have to treat this differently, with sensitivity and a lot of care. Not only are their faces ruined, but so are their lives. Not to mention the damage this must be doing to successful, lucrative careers."

"And you think I'm sensitive?" He asked with a slight complimentary chuckle.

"Yes. You are very sensitive and passionate, especially regarding matters that concern minorities—the disenfranchised. Pat, I haven't forgotten the fund-raiser you organized for Tom Brown. Let's face it, how many lawyers actually back a Black senator? You know . . ." A thought struck her. "That's sort of when this whole thing got started—at that event."

Pat's brow rose. "Excuse me?"

"Dr. Zimmerman was there. That's where Ms. Griffin met him. He bumped into her—supposedly on accident— then he dazzled her with tales of caramel-colored beauty."

"Hmm. I don't recall that name being on the guest list. Are you sure?"

"Positive. Pat—" A cold chill swept through her. "Do you think he talked to others that night? That room was filled with wealthy, influential Black people . . .

"Oh my God," she whispered. "Pat, wasn't it shortly after this fund-raiser that Senator Brown dropped his campaign?"

Pat's face registered surprise. "It was."

"You didn't find out what happened, why he dropped out?"

"No. I was so angry and humiliated that I took it personally. I did receive a form letter of apology and thanks for our support. They returned the money we raised. "

"Well, maybe this Dr. Zimmerman got to him too."

Chapter 3

For weeks, she worked tirelessly, forsaking any semblance of a social life in search for justice. She put in twelve hour days, along with her very competent secretary and assistant, Valerie. God bless her, Danithia thought, as she handed Valerie yet another draft with cut-and-pasted text and handwritten changes all over it. She admired Valerie as she watched her struggle through the document without ever complaining.

Valerie was a godsend. She was also African American, an extremely intelligent, slightly overweight secretary whom Danithia had hired despite the office manager's encouragement to pick another candidate. The other, "better," candidate was a gorgeous blond, blue-eyed woman who looked more interested in her personal appearance than she would ever be in making sure Danithia's needs were taken care of. In contrast, the instant Danithia and Valerie met, they had an amicable rapport. It was almost as if the two of them had immediately made a silent vow to each other, "I'll watch your back, if you watch mine."

Since the very first day of Valerie's employment, Danithia had been relying upon her, and frankly, her sharp mind, accuracy, and speedy fingers on a keyboard had saved Danithia, helping her make outrageous deadlines on more than one occasion. They were a team. Valerie was protective and discreet. She was always polite and friendly, but she had a way of letting you know just how far to go with her, drawing lines that you couldn't see but could feel.

Behind Danithia's closed office door, they would talk like girlfriends, intimately sharing in each other's lives. And behind closed doors, they would call each other "girl" and "girlfriend" and use euphemisms that others in the office would probably gape at in surprise. Secretaries were rarely this friendly with their superiors.

Danithia made a mental note to be very generous to Valerie this year at Christmas.

"Good night, Valerie," Danithia said, feeling a little guilty for leaving her.

"Good night, Danithia."

"Hey, thanks for staying late to finish this. I'll be in around five or six in the morning to do revisions that will be on your desk when you get here at nine. Remember, we want to file this with the court tomorrow. Okay?"

"Sure, no problem. It's going faster than I thought it would. I'll be done in less than an hour, I think," Valerie said while still pounding the keyboard.

Danithia glanced at the computer screen and noted that Valerie hadn't even made a typo. "You go girl!" Danithia said, raised her hand for a high five, and the two women slapped palms and shared a laugh.

~ ~ ~

Danithia's heels echoed loudly against the concrete of the garage floor as she rushed to her new car. When she saw it sitting there, all shiny and new, black and sleek, she felt a rush of pride and success by just looking at it. Her friends had urged her to get rid of her sensible Volkswagen Rabbit and buy a "real" car, a classy car, a car that would reflect her success. And she had to admit that this Lexus certainly reflected something. Danithia had it trimmed in gold, and the effects were stunning. Sometimes she wondered if the car was too much—too flashy. But those thoughts would always flee the minute she slid behind the wheel and floated to her various destinations.

Danithia approached the car, circling it to get in on the driver's side. She stopped abruptly when she noticed an ugly, long scratch from door to bumper. She gasped. Someone or something had horribly marred the finish with a long, deep, ugly groove, which, upon closer inspection, looked like it had been made with a key or some other sharp, jagged object. It was the kind of scratch angry women sometimes put on the cars of their former lovers. But Danithia did not, at present, have a lover. And her beautiful car was ruined. I cannot believe someone did this. But someone had. A thought occurred to her and she rushed back inside the building, furiously punching the elevator button.

Danithia stomped up to the security desk. Somebody's going to pay for this, she inwardly seethed.

"May I help you?"

Suddenly Danithia was face-to-face with a very impressive, broad-shouldered, dark-chocolate brother she had never seen, with a voice as velvety and deep as any singer. For a moment she lost her entire train of thought and her anger seeped away like a rapidly deflating balloon.

"I . . . I work in the building and I just came from the garage and someone has scratched my car," Danithia said, sounding like a petulant child even to herself.

"I'm sorry to hear that, ma'am. Let's go take a look at it. I'll need to make a report."

His penetrating look and gentle, deep voice, again surprised her. Danithia realized a second too late that she was staring. This man is fine! Where has he been hiding? I've never seen him before. What a beautiful smile!

"My incident report will be useful to you when you make a claim with your insurance company," he explained while gathering a clipboard and pen.

"I just bought this car and I hate to make a claim if I don't have to. Doesn't the building take responsibility for vandalism done on its premises?" Danithia asked, knowing full well they probably didn't.

She noticed his smile again, one that made her heart do a two-step dance inside her chest. It was a promising smile. A welcome.

"I doubt it, ma'am, but I'll check for you." He reached for her elbow and with a light, somehow sensual touch, he gently guided her to the elevators. Again Danithia was struck by his size, judging him to be about six feet and three or four inches, broad of shoulder and muscular. He smiled easily, and he was a complete gentlemen, allowing her to enter the elevator first. His cologne was rich and fragrant, the kind of scent that follows a man as he passes you by, his scent enticingly hanging in the air long after he's gone. Danithia almost asked him what he was wearing.

"I'm new to the building security team, and unfortunately I'm not fully aware of the procedures for this sort of thing, but trust me, I'll take care of you."

Take care of me. Danithia liked the way that sounded coming from his lips. Surprised at her own thoughts and peculiar feelings, she attributed this uncharacteristic sexual attraction to the strain of a very long, hard day.

"Well, I appreciate anything you can do to help," she said. "I'm just so surprised that this sort of thing happened."

"Are you positive it happened here? I mean, did you go out during the lunch hour or anything?"

"No, I've been in the building all day. I haven't moved the car, and a scratch this bad I would have noticed this morning. Besides, at home I keep my car parked in my garage, and there's no one there to lay a finger on it," she explained, realizing that she was talking too fast and probably saying too much to this stranger.

"Okay, then it probably happened here. Which car is yours ma'am?" He asked.

She pointed to the black Lexus, and a sudden feeling of guilt for its obvious pretentiousness gripped her.

He, however, did not flinch, act offended or impressed by the car. Now she really did feel stupid for feeling guilty. This man could care less what kind of car she was driving, and furthermore, why the hell did she care what he thought anyway.

"Looks like somebody did a job on you." He squatted to get a better look.

He lightly caressed the scratch. She noticed his hands. His nails were short, clean, and manicured. The hair on the top of his head was beginning to thin, and she suddenly remembered her father's favorite phrase when he was starting to bald, "Girl, your daddy's gettin' a hole in his natural!" And she almost giggled.

He stood and readjusted his pants that had risen and were squeezing his muscular, upper thighs. He towered over her, staring intently at her face. He seemed to be studying her eyes.

Danithia blinked several times and thought about stepping back, but didn't. For some reason, instead of feeling intimidated by his height and bulk, she was strangely comforted by it. As if he was her appointed guardian angel, her teddy bear, and he was here to protect her. I am definitely tripping, she told herself.

"I'll fill out this report for you. Your name?"

"Oh—I'm sorry. My name is Danithia Gilberts."

Instead of writing it down, he tucked the clipboard under his arm and gently, but firmly, shook her hand.

"I'm Alex Powers. Pleasure to meet you."

He continued to gently pump her arm up and down, shaking it longer than usual, and his grip and smile captivated her for a moment.

"Nice—very nice to meet you, too. Thank you for helping me with this."

"No problem. That's what I'm here for. Now, let's get this form completed so you can be on your way. It is getting late."

He pulled his hand away, and she felt the warmth—a glow where his hand had been—starting to fade. He asked questions which Danithia answered in a hesitant voice. For some unknown reason she felt like she was in a fog, hypnotized or something. She couldn't explain it if someone had asked. What was going on with her at that moment? He asked the questions, Danithia answered, but she felt disconnected, disoriented. Her eyes were glued to his lips—full, generous lips, the kind of lips you know can set you in a fit! She couldn't stop staring.

Finally, she pulled her eyes away and studied his entire face, now gripped in concentration. His jawline was square, his skin dark and smooth. A true African nose, wide and flat. But his eyes—his eyes were like dark pools that seemed to ripple and sparkle with intrigue and mystery. His forehead was wide and generous. Nicely finishing off his face were cheekbones that plump when he smiled, giving him a boyish look. And he smiled often, showing beautiful, even white teeth. He was sucking a butterscotch drop and when he talked he expelled butterscotch breath. Suddenly, she craved a butterscotch-laced kiss.

What is wrong with me! She stepped back as if she had been pushed by an unseen hand. Her heel caught on something. Her ankle twisted, gave, and yelping at the pain, she went down, her bottom hit the pavement with a horrible whack. She felt totally stupid.

Too late, Alex reached for her, eyes wide with shock and concern.

"Wait. Let me check your ankle before you stand up." Alex's huge hands encircled her ankle. He rotated it ever so gently, gazing at her, asking in his mesmerizing voice if she felt any pain. At the moment, the only thing she felt was a longing for him to continue touching her, holding her leg slightly up, caressing her ankle.

"Do you think you can stand on it?" Alex asked, noticing her wince.

"Yes, I think so. Let me try to stand."

"Here, let me help you up." Alex placed his hands under the pit of her arms and, as if she were a feather, lifted her. His hands settled on her waist to help steady her, and she had the most incredible urge to turn around and embrace him. Instead, she pushed herself away.

The two of them stared at each other, tension rising between them. A woman's voice interrupted this moment of intense appraisal.

"Danithia, what's going on? Are you all right?" Valerie asked, approaching them with a look of pure curiosity on her face.

"Someone scratched my car, and he was doing a report, and then I slipped and fell," Danithia said too quickly, sounding overwhelmed.

"Hi," Alex said to Valerie but he kept looking at Danithia with concern.

"Hi." Valerie took the time to do a quick once over of Alex, then turned Danithia and asked, "Can you drive? Did you hurt your foot or something?"

"I'm okay, just a little startled is all." Danithia turned to Alex. "Are we finished with the report? I really need to get going."

"Yes, ma'am. I've got all the information I need—I mean—that the building management will need to handle this situation." His tone was professional and serious, quite different from the one she'd heard before Valerie arrived.

"Okay then. Thank you for all your help." She reached for the door but he stopped her, his hand briefly covering hers. She noticed that her hand completely disappeared inside his larger one.

"Let me." He opened the car door, and Danithia carefully slid in. That new-car smell permeated the air and again she felt embarrassed at her extravagance in purchasing this car, leather interior, gold trimming, and all.

"Danithia, please call me when you get home. I'd like to know you made it okay," Valerie called, looking from Danithia to Alex with a what's-going-on-here look upon her face.

"Okay, I'll do that. You drive carefully too, Val."

Danithia took one last look at Mr. Alex Powers, with his fine self, flashed her most sensual smile, and drove off.

~ ~ ~

At the first stop light, Danithia adjusted the rearview mirror so she could look at her face. She saw a woman who looked a little disheveled, hair a little out of place, and eyes that looked strange. She tucked and smoothed her hair, licked her lips to smooth the lipstick and tried to understand the look in her eyes. Her thoughts swung back to Alex and she wondered who he was—if he was married.

He sure did look nice, and his voice, oh, his voice was like velvet, smooth, deep, sensual. He was very articulate and clean cut. In fact, he really didn't look like a security officer at all. Something about him seemed out of place, like he really didn't belong there. Danithia allowed her imagination to run away, and she enjoyed playing this guessing game with herself. Admitting the unusual effect he had on her was refreshing. It was rare for Danithia to act like a schoolgirl upon first meeting a man, but this man did something to her. I felt something, she thought.

~ ~ ~

She had barely entered the house before she heard the shrill ringing of the telephone. She started to limp on her way to answering it.

"Hello." She slipped off her shoes, softly caressing her injured ankle.

"Hi, Danithia. It's Valerie. I thought you were going to call me when you got home. What happened?"

"I just got home, Parnelle Jones!" she joked, referring to the well-known race car driver. "I'll call you back as soon as I let Tanya out. Okay?"

"Don't forget."

"I won't.

Danithia's golden retriever jumped up and down, trying desperately to get her attention. She put the telephone back in its cradle and immediately was assaulted by the dog she loved. Tanya licked her face and hands while her tail whipped furiously back and forth. This was the welcome home ritual that Danithia enjoyed every night.

"Hey girl, how ya doing? Huh, how's my girl?" she crooned as the dog continued to jiggle and dance and slobber everywhere.

"Wanna go for a walk? Huh girl, walk?" The dog instantly recognized those words and raced to where

Danithia kept a leash hanging on a nail near the refrigerator. Tanya sat down, as she was taught to do, and waited for Danithia to hook the leash to her collar.

"Can I put my tennis shoes on?" Danithia said as she walked to the sofa with Tanya on her heels. Her ankle hurt so bad she really didn't want to take Tanya out, but she knew she had to. She was barely able to put on her white socks and Nike sneakers, her ankle was very tender to the touch. She didn't bother changing clothes, simply slipped off her suit jacket and grabbed Tanya's leash. Tanya leaped out the door as soon as Danithia opened it.

"Hey, slow down will ya!" she shouted at Tanya, something she always had to do when they first started their evening walk. Tanya was so anxious to go outside after being cooped up all day, it seemed to take her awhile before she remembered her training. Though Danithia loved her dog, this was one thing about her that always irritated her. For the first five minutes of every walk, they'd tug and pull and battle one another before Tanya would settle down and prance around, sniffing everything in sight, finally she would do her business and the two of them could go back inside and enjoy a quiet evening together.

Danithia thought about her life, how boring and predictable it was. Frankly, if it weren't for the interesting cases she had to work on, there would not be much for her to look forward to each day. Loving a dog just wasn't enough. She never seemed to meet eligible bachelors who were able to stimulate her mind, much less her libido. And after several years of disappointing suitors, she had all but given up on love.

As Danithia and Tanya walked, she thought again about the steamy romance novels that Patricia Griffin wrote and marveled at the woman's imagination. She knew that Patricia did not involve herself romantically with men, so how she managed to write such thought-provoking love stories intrigued her. Then she thought about Alex and tried to sort out what, if anything, her reaction to him today might have meant. She knew she was lonely, but at the same time she also led a fulfilling, active life. She had good friends and plenty of family members to be with. So, why did it now feel like it was no longer enough?

Alex had touched her, literally and figuratively. It was as simple as that. His eyes talked to her. His smile caressed her face. And it left her feeling—wanting—more. But he was a complete stranger. A security guard. But for reasons she couldn't understand, she didn't care. Her family would probably frown on it. Her father, never thinking anyone good enough for his baby girl, would not like him. Her brothers, all three of them, were overly protective and at times had literally run possible suitors away with their intimidating stares and personal questions. She hated taking a new man to meet them, but duty called—her duty to please her family. And she always did what they asked, even when she knew better. The outcome was usually the same. No one would like her new love interest but her and, of course, her mother. This time, she thought, if I get a chance to go out with Alex, or any other man, I'm not taking him home!

She crossed her arms, lost in thought, as she stopped to allow Tanya to do her business. It was now very dark, slivers of the moon's light her only guide. Her vision was not very clear, but when she looked to her left, she seemed to be staring straight at Alex. He was sitting in a parked car, the reflection of a nearby street light slightly illuminated him, just a few yards away. Her mouth opened and closed, and she blinked in surprise. Alex? Was her mind playing tricks on her? Alex? Impossible.

She yanked Tanya's chain, but the dog did not budge. She screamed, "Come on!" She tried to run in the direction of the parked car, but her injured ankle rebelled. Suddenly bright lights came on, blinding her. She raised a hand to shield her eyes. In that same instant, the car made an illegal U-turn and sped away.

Danithia gasped for breath, her heart jumping wildly in her chest. She gingerly placed her hand against it, breathing rapidly, willing herself to calm down. Excited, Tanya jumped up on her, probably thinking they were playing some kind of game. Danithia pushed her down. "Bad dog!" She yelled, in a dry, frog-like tone, wincing as her ankle began to throb again.

Was that Alex? She wondered again. How did he know where I live? Then she remembered all the personal information she had given him for the incident report. How could I be so stupid! She smacked a palm upside her head. I told him everything about me. Is he stalking me?

No, she chided herself. He couldn't be. Why would he?

A thousand questions raced through her mind as she returned home. Instinct told her to check and lock all doors and windows. Funny, how thoughts of amour quickly became those of possible danger. The phone rang, and she jumped. She stared at it, afraid to pick it up. After several rings, she listened to her own voice politely ask the caller to leave a message and she'd get back to them as soon as possible. Then the beep.

"Now, how long does it take to let a dog out? Huh?"

It was Valerie. Danithia snatched the phone from the receiver.

"I'm here. I'm here."

"Why do you sound like you're out of breath?"

"Umm, just ..." She wasn't sure if she should mention to Valerie what she thought had just happened.

"What's wrong with you?" Valerie said, sounding slightly annoyed.

"Nothing, just came back inside from walking Tanya. I guess I was thinking about something else."

"Wellll," Valerie said, dragging out the word, fishing for answers. "Don't keep me in suspense. What happened tonight? And did I catch the right vibes, was that guy flirting with you?"

"I'm not sure what you're talking about. He was just helping me with my car. Did you see that scratch?" she asked, her voice rising.

"Yeah, I saw it. Looked pretty bad. What are you going to do about it?"

"I'm not sure ..."

"Who do you think did it? I mean that looked deliberate to me."

"I have no idea, but whoever it was needs a good ass whipping."

"Sho you right!" Valerie replied. "But anyway, enough about your damn car. Who was that guy? Girlfriend, he looked mighty fine. I'd like to get with him, if you know what I mean."

"You need to stop. He's security. Just started, I gather. He seemed very nice, and he was very helpful."

"Helpful, my behind. He looked like he was checking you out, Danithia."

"Do you think so?" she asked, her voice sounding alarmed. "What did you see, Valerie? Tell me, what made you say that?" She almost shouted.

"Calm down girl. Has it been so long you forgot what flirting looks like?"

"No!"

"Girl, what is wrong with you, stuttering and stammering like you can't talk? What's up?"

Danithia hesitated for a moment, but then she decided she needed help figuring this thing out.

"Listen, I know this is going to sound crazy, but I think I just saw him, watching me as I walked Tanya."

"Saw who? The security guy! Are you kidding?"

"No . . . I mean . . . oh God, he scared me half to death. I couldn't really see, but I think it was him, and when I ran toward the car, it took off. He damn near ran me over!"

"Girl, this is serious. Are you sure it was him?"

"Well, fairly sure. I don't know, it was kind of dark."

"This is what I think we should do. I'm going to call the building right now, see if he's there. What's his name?"

"Alex. I think he said Alex."

"Okay. You sit tight, and I'll call you right back."

Danithia paced the floor, while Tanya followed her every movement with her sorrowful eyes. It couldn't have been him, was all Danithia could chant to herself.

"He's there." Valerie said the moment Danithia picked up the phone.

"He is! Thank god. Did you talk to him?"

"No. I just asked to speak to him and the guy said hold on a moment. I figured he was going to get him, so I hung up."

"Hmm," Danithia said. "So you really didn't speak to him."

"No, but the guy went to get him, so he must have been there."

"Well, maybe." Danithia was still not sure if she should believe her eyes or her ears.

"Danithia, why would that man be watching you? Huh? Think about it."

Danithia was silent for a moment, wondering and replaying the scene again in her mind.

"You're probably right," she said, finally conceded. "Why would he watch me? I'm getting paranoid in my old age."

"Sho you right! Danithia, can I ask you something?"

"Sure, you know you can."

"Okay, let's say it wasn't him you saw tonight. And let's also say that he was interested in you. Would you go out with him?"

"Would I go out with him!" she repeated, her tone incredulous. "Just a few moments ago I thought he was stalking me!"

"Yeah, but he wasn't."

"We don't know that for sure."

"Danithia?"

"What?"

"Stop stalling and answer the question."

"I don't know if I'd go out with him. Maybe. Would you?"

"Definitely! Boyfriend was fine! But, he saw you first."

"Valerie, p-leeze!"

"You know what, Danithia? You should go after what you really want."

"And what do I really want, Val, since you seem to think you know?"

"You want love. Plain and simple. Being alone at night is no fun. And whatever form love comes in should not be an issue. Not if you're smart."

"What's that supposed to mean?"

"He's security, you're an attorney. It doesn't take a genius to figure out there's a pretty big gap between your career aspirations."

"Look, why are we even discussing this? We don't know anything about that guy. Shoot, he might be married, or engaged—"

"Gay or— " Valerie interrupted.

"Yeah, gay or living with somebody. You are definitely jumping the gun on this one."

"Maybe. But I could find out for you. It wouldn't hurt for me to ask."

"Suit yourself, but Val—"

"What?"

"I'm really not interested."

"Yeah right. That's why you fell and busted your behind when cupid goosed you by landing on your shoulder. And now you're seeing him when he's not even there. You can hide if you want to, girlfriend, but it won't work for long."

"Are you through with your assumptions?" Danithia said with a chuckle.

"I guess so. For now anyway. Goodnight, Danithia. I'll see you tomorrow."

~ ~ ~

Valerie was right. When you're alone at night, lying in bed, it would be nice to have somebody to hold you, someone to help calm your spirit. Danithia tossed and turned all night long thinking about her longing, her loneliness. For some reason, she could not get comfortable. Visions of Alex kept bouncing through her head. Her mind kept replaying his touch, the warmth of his hand, its smoothness, and his voice, a very nice voice. Like music to her ears. She yanked the covers again, and they completely came untucked from the corners, something she could not stand. Jumping out of bed, furious at herself, she secured the sheet. Feelings of frustration assaulted her as she tried to figure out what was wrong with her. Lonely, that's what she was. Lonely. It was as simple as it was complex. Ears raised, Tanya watched her. The dog turned her head to the side as if waiting for a question to be put before her. Danithia bent to pet her, looked into her eyes, eyes that seemed to understand the master's frustration.

"It's okay, Tanya. Your master is just a little weird tonight. Go back to sleep."

She sat on the floor beside her dog, who lovingly placed her head in her lap. Danithia stroked her, talked soothingly to the dog, thinking it sure would be nice to be talking to a human being right now, someone who could advise her, help calm the sea of raw emotions ebbing and flowing deep inside her.

Eventually she climbed back into bed, attempting to get some sleep before the alarm sounded. Danithia noticed the time. It was 1:58 a.m. Sighing her now familiar sigh, she realized that there was nothing to do but wait for blessed sleep to claim her, plunge her into total darkness and unconsciousness, where she could escape her fears—and her desires.

Running. She is running. Running and crying. Running from something she cannot see. Her arms are extended as if trying to embrace something as tears stream down her face. Her fingers open and close, flex and reach. But nothing appears in them. Whatever she is reaching for, she is unable to grasp. And then she faintly smells butterscotch. She sniffs the air around her and smiles. She wants some butterscotch. Then she hears music and voices.

Abruptly, Danithia awakened from her dream. The morning news blared from the radio. The dream was so real. Never before had she believed it possible to smell things in a dream, but this time she definitely did. She smelled butterscotch so clearly that she actually craved it right now. Then she thought about Alex, his kissable lips, broad shoulders, his inviting smile. Damn! She had it bad.

~ ~ ~

"Danithia," Valerie's voice came over the intercom. "It's Mr. Security Officer on the line."

"Who?" Danithia asked absently, totally immersed in research for her new case.

"The guy downstairs, the security officer who helped you last night—Alex—he's on the line. You want to take the call?"

"Of course, put him through."

She pulled off her clip earring, lifted the receiver, her head cocked to one side, and for reasons she didn't quite understand, she was smiling.

"Danithia Gilberts speaking."

"Good afternoon, Ms. Gilberts. This is Officer Powers. I'm following up on the incident with your car."

"Yes."

"The building management has a limited liability policy with respect to damage incurred on the premises. The policy in essence states that you park at your own risk, and they do not take responsibility for any loss or damage incurred to any vehicle or its contents while parked on the premises," Alex recited.

"Well, I'm not surprised. But I was hoping that because I reported the damage before I left the parking lot, my claim might be covered."

"That would be correct if the damage was caused through some fault of the building—like something from the building fell on it and damaged it—otherwise we have no liability. I'm sorry." He added, "Now, if you can prove that an object did the damage, then we would handle the claim, ma'am."

"Please, you can drop the ma'am and just call me Danithia. Okay?"

"Okay. And you can call me Alex."

"Good. I have to admit that I doubted the building would cover it anyway. So, Alex, do you have any suggestions as to where to get that scratch fixed?" she asked, using her "helpless female" voice. She knew perfectly well where to get the damage repaired she just wanted to talk to him some more. Suddenly, she felt better than she had all day. Just hearing his voice seemed to lift her spirits. She felt as if she was floating—floating on billowy clouds of softness. She felt somehow peaceful as they spoke. Funny, but listening to Alex's voice reminded her of so many pleasurable things. Its sensual tone soothed her the way a warm spring breeze would. Sudden visions of her childhood swing came to her mind, that gentle back and forth motion that used to lull her into sweet surrender, slumber, and eventual sleep. She closed her eyes and began to sway. None of the fear she had felt last night even crossed her mind now.

"May I ask you a personal question?" Alex asked.

"Well, that depends on how personal you're planning to get. Let's just say I'll reserve the right to answer that question until I hear the question you're planning to ask," Danithia said, smiling.

"Are you married?"

"No, I'm not. Are you?" Danithia countered.

"No."

There was a few seconds of utter silence.

"Why do you ask, Alex?"

"Would you be interested in having lunch with me someday soon?"

"That sounds nice. I'd like that. When?"

"I'm off tomorrow. Could we meet at the Tabor Center?"

"Let me check my calendar. How about 12:30?"

"Great. I'll meet you in front of the food court, by the cooker counter."

"See you tomorrow, then." Danithia's stomach fluttered at the thought of being close to him again so soon. She felt no fear of him now but knew she must make sure it wasn't him she saw last night. Somehow, she must find a way to broach the subject.

Chapter 4

*A*lex ran the sharp edge of the razor over his jaw, then stroked upward rhythmically, all the while he hummed. His mind replayed his conversation with Danithia. He smiled when he thought about how easily she had agreed to meet him for lunch. She wasn't a stuck-up, boojee, wanna-be White lawyer. That surprised him—intrigued him actually.

Ever since he met her, she had been on his mind. He wanted to know more about her—more than the general stuff he'd been told. He wondered if she liked chocolate, sunsets, long walks, the majestic Rocky Mountains, or did she prefer the quiet serenity of running, clear streams? Did she like love slow and easy or unbridled, furious, full of passion? He normally did not wonder about such things at the outset of meeting a woman, but this one—well, this one was different. From the flash of anger—the fire—he'd seen in her eyes, up close and personal, to her sudden surrender to him by nothing more than his simple smile.

Power. He felt powerful, almost almighty, especially when he had watched her walk her frisky dog. He admired the strength of her well-formed muscular legs, her firm round behind, even the slight jiggle of her small breasts. He was admiring her so much that it almost got him caught. He shook his head now, realizing how stupid he had been. His so-called covert appraisal of her was almost blown. Fortunately for him her dog didn't immediately obey her command to run, so intent was he or she to continue sniffing another dog's poop. He laughed aloud then, remembering that for a split second Danithia looked like a beautiful deer caught in bright lights. He didn't laugh because he thought it was humorous, because it wasn't. It was just that some things have a way of striking you as funny, even when they aren't. No, to the contrary, he sincerely hoped he hadn't frightened her. Trust. That was what he needed to build. She must trust him with all her heart, mind, and soul. If not, all could be lost.

~ ~ ~

She saw him first as she ascended the long escalator to the top of Tabor Center. He was standing just outside the food court. She noticed that he had dressed up for her. Dark green silk shirt, opened slightly at his throat, beige slacks with a hard, well-defined crease, and loafers. His hands were in his pockets and he rocked slightly. It seemed to her as if he was trying hard not to be, or look, anxious. She was. Something about his physical presence was commanding yet comforting. If she could see auras, like one of her friends claimed to be able to do, she imagined she would see purple or royal blue squiggly lines bouncing and radiating off him, as if he were royalty. This kind of assessment of a man was outrageous for her. She almost never put this much thought or speculation into the character of any man, much less one she had just met.

"Hi."

"Hello," he replied with a heart-stopping smile. "Hungry?"

"Yes, very. Didn't get any breakfast this morning."

"That's not good," he replied. "You know breakfast is the most important meal of the day."

"You don't say!"

He smiled. "You're a lawyer, I'm sure you already know such an elementary thing."

"That I do," she said, chuckling.

He looked around at all the various eateries. "What would you like?"

"Mmmm, cookies! Don't they smell delicious. I love their butter cookies," she said, pointing at the cookie stand.

"Well then let's start with dessert. Cookies it is."

She gave him a puzzled look. "Are you kidding?"

"Counselor," he said using a serious tone and holding his hand as if it were gripping a microphone. "Can you cite for me a precedent or case law that unequivocally states that dessert cannot and will not be consumed before the main course?" He put the fictitious microphone before her lips.

"No, Your Honor," she said, laughing at him. "I cannot cite such a case."

"Then," he said, taking her hand and guiding her toward the cookie counter, "we shall start with dessert!"

He gripped her hand and together they marched up to the cashier as if they were on a most important mission. As they approached the counter, they were both laughing.

"Hey, you sounded pretty good, almost had me thinking I was talking to a judge."

"I may be just a security officer to you, but I read extensively, and I watch the legal dramas on television. I can imitate almost anybody."

"You're a regular Tommy Davidson, huh?"

"Not quite. What kind of cookies do you want?"

"Butter! The bite-size ones...three of those and three chocolate, chocolate chip."

"You like chocolate," he said. "I knew it!"

~ ~ ~

They both decided to try something new, so they selected Filipino cuisine. He ordered the beef, she the chicken. As they sat down, she looked at him towering over her, and a sudden feeling of overwhelming curiosity came over her.

"Smells good," he commented.

"Yeah, and it looks good too. . . ready?"

"Ready," he said, showing mock fear.

"You go first," she said.

"I don't think so, young lady. You wanted to be adventurous and I followed you like a fool. Now, what's proper is for you to go first."

"Chicken!" she teased him.

"Ain't no shame in my game."

She scooped up a generous portion of rice and started to put it in her mouth.

"Uh, uh. Not the rice, I wanna see you eat some meat!"

She looked up at him and smiled. "Okay." She cut a small portion of the chicken, poised it over her mouth for a second or two, then plunged the fork inside. She gasped, her eyes crossed and then she slowly slumped to one side of her chair. Her head hung forward.

Then, smiling, she sat up and chewed the food. "Delicious!" she exclaimed.

"Damn, woman, I thought they done up and killed yo ass!" he said, laughing. "Don't ever do that again," he added trying to sound serious. "You've got to remember one thing."

"And what might that be?"

"In this relationship, I'm the comedian."

"Can't handle a little competition, huh?" she replied as she digested the word "relationship" and wondered what the hell he was talking about. Lunch is not a relationship.

"Did you call that little fainting scene competition? That was downright pitiful."

"I had you going, don't lie, you know I did."

He looked down at his plate, looked up again, and said with a serious tone. "You did have me going. My heart was beating real fast, still is in fact. Feel." He took her hand and placed it over his heart.

Through the cool silk fabric, warmth radiated, and his heart was indeed beating hard and fast and for a moment she felt bad. But the sensation of his hand firmly pressed against hers, the warmth of his chest, swept away all feelings of remorse and replaced them with feelings of something else.

"Ohhhh," she crooned. "I'm sorry." She kissed his cheek and looked into his eyes.

"I'd feel much better if you'd plant that kiss right here." He tapped his lips with her finger.

"Now, your Honor," she said teasingly. "I think that would be a tad bit inappropriate, don't you?"

"Probably. I don't want your Filipino chicken breath on me anyway."

She burst out laughing. "You're too much, you know that?"

"Yeah, been told that a time or two. Anyway, tell me about you."

She watched him place a very large piece of meat in his mouth. And she wondered if he were more interested in her or the food.

"I'm working on a very interesting case right now. I can't mention a lot of the details, no names or anything too specific, but let's just say it's going to set the African American community smack-dab in the middle of more controversy."

"Controversy? Sounds interesting."

"Do you have any siblings?"

"Yep, a brother and a sister."

"Do you guys favor each other, you know, look alike?"

"Not really. You can see a family resemblance, but we each have a uniqueness about us. Why do you ask?"

"Part of this case is about how you look, how you perceive others think of how you look, and acceptance of who you are."

"You lost me."

"Okay. I'd venture to say that all of us at one time or another have experienced issues with color, you know, light skin versus dark."

"Oh, sure. In fact, my sister is so high yellow we make her sit in the sun, she's too damn bright!"

"Exactly," she speared a bit of chicken. "That's the kind of thing I'm talking about. I have a client who was so unhappy with her dark skin that she did something really drastic."

"What'd she do?"

"She tried to lighten it."

"How?"

"Can you believe, she let somebody put chemicals on her, chemicals that didn't work?"

"Chemicals in your hair, chemicals on the face, what's the difference?" he said jokingly. "She's still dark, huh?"

"No." She spoke with sadness. "But I bet she wishes she were."

"She's not dead, is she?"

"No, but . . . she's very badly hurt, and my heart goes out to her and everybody else involved in this mess."

"It's a bunch of people?"

"I'm not sure yet. We're still investigating, trying to find victims."

"Ambulance chasing?"

"No!" she said indignant. "That's unethical, and I don't handle my cases in any way to jeopardize myself or my firm."

He put up his hands as if warding off blows. "Sorry, didn't mean to imply that you were unethical. I just wondered how you guys go about finding victims."

"It can be a complicated, delicate situation, especially with this particular case."

"I really don't mean to sound insensitive, but people who do stuff like that, well, in my humble opinion, they get what they deserve."

"At first I thought the same thing. Then, I met my client, and she is a victim. I talked to her, am getting to know her and gaining an understanding of why she felt compelled to do such a thing to herself. And I'd venture to say that her story is neither unique, nor is it something lots of other people of African descent haven't thought about doing at one time or another. The reason behind this kind of action is very sad."

He stared at her and it felt almost like waves of her compassion were radiating off her, and he could really feel what she was saying.

"You can't judge anybody until you've walked in their shoes. And I mean that literally," Danithia continued.

"I guess you're right. When I was younger, believe it or not, I was a skinny kid, tall and skinny, with big feet."

"Sure can't tell that from looking at you now," she said, admiring his physique.

"Don't let the muscles fool you. I got so tired of people teasing me, I decided to bulk up. You know...what's the worst thing that happened to me?"

"No, what?"

"Kids used to call me Jesus Christ."

"Excuse me?"

"They said my feet were so big, I could walk on water."

She couldn't help herself, she fell out laughing until tears came running down her cheeks. He laughed, too.

"Told you I was the comedian 'round this camp!" He said, and sipped his soda.

With that she laughed even harder.

"But let me stop playing," he said. "We were talking about something very serious. Your client. How is she doing?"

"Overall, not very good. There are implications here that are so far-reaching that they are intimidating."

"Can't be that bad?"

"Oh no? Let's do a little exercise."

"No, thanks, not while I'm eating. Exercise is not good for the digestion."

"Come on now, seriously."

"Okay. I'll be serious."

"Imagine you're wealthy."

"Oh, I can do that."

"And you've decided to become, uhh, let's say, a woman."

"Now you're barking up the wrong tree!"

"Hear me out. You're a wealthy, well-known Black man in the community. You're successful and sought after. Now, you done gone and turned yourself into a woman! How do you think that would affect your business, your wealth, hell, your social life?"

"I suspect I'd have a lot more men friends," he said using a feminine voice and gesturing with a limp wrist.

"Be serious." She slapped his wrist hanging in the air. "How do you think that kind of change would affect you financially? Do you think all the people who did business with you before will continue to do business with you after?"

"Not the self-righteous ones. And that may just be the majority."

"Exactly. But on a smaller scale, I'd venture to say that my clients are experiencing some horrible backlash as a result of their actions. Not everybody is going to take the time to try and understand why they did what they did. You see what I mean by overpowering implications and consequences they collectively face?"

"Yeah, I do. That's deep."

"Deeper than I could ever have imagined. I want so bad to help them, but it's going to be hard."

"I have faith in your ability to rise to the occasion."

"It's not really about me. But thanks for the vote of confidence."

"If it's not about the competence of their lawyer, what is it about?"

"There are issues I can't begin to touch. For instance, I can't bring back their dignity, or their pride. I can't make business associates trust their judgment again. I can't make them whole, physically or mentally. All I can do is try to get them monetary compensation. And . . . well, I just don't feel like that's going to be enough."

"It's a start," Alex said. "The rest will come with time. The healing process is slow. It has to be. They will take tiny steps back to where they used to be, financially and otherwise. You've got to believe that and not fret too much about the rest. After all it is, by your own admission, out of your hands."

She sat quietly for a moment, absorbing his thoughtful words and the profound insight he showed. She looked up and smiled at him. Searching his face, she saw one of the funniest and kindest men she'd been with in a long, long time.

"Thank you for saying that. Now, tell me more about you."

"What would you like to know?"

"Have you ever been married?"

"Yes, once," he said. "My ex-wife and I were married for a short time, only three years. It turned out not to be a match made in heaven."

"I'm sorry to hear it didn't work out."

"Don't be, I'm not."

"Any children?"

"No," he replied, a bit of sorrow in his voice. "You know, you have the most beautiful smile." He said, changing the subject.

"Thank you."

"You're welcome. If I can make you smile like that, I'll do it every chance I get. And that, my dear," he paused to cradle her hand in his, "is a promise."

~ ~ ~

They left the Tabor Center and walked along the 16th Street Mall, stopping occasionally to admire various window displays of the major department stores. In one particular window there was a mirrored background, and they could clearly see themselves standing there. He, so tall and broad shouldered, and she was almost as tall, wearing high-heeled shoes, her slender physique greatly contrasted with his bulkier one.

"We look good together," he commented.

"You think so?"

"Yeah, I do."

He turned to face her, reached for her hand, while his face took on a very serious demeanor.

"Danithia, I'd very much like to see you again. Would you consider going to dinner and a play with me?"

"Of course I would. I enjoyed our time together today, too."

"Have you ever heard of the Delany Sisters?"

"Yes."

"The play that chronicles their lives is opening next Saturday night. I'd like to get tickets."

"Isn't it called 'Having Our Say?'"

"Yeah, that's it. I know a nice restaurant we could have dinner either before or after the play, your choice."

"How about after?"

"I was hoping you'd say that."

She smiled, and he smiled too.

"I could stand here all day, just lookin' at you," he said.

"I could too, but," she said and glanced at her watch, "duty calls. I've got to get back."

"I understand. Do you mind if I walk with you?"

"No. Why would I mind?"

"I just didn't want to be presumptuous, that's why I asked."

"What lady wouldn't want a man as handsome as you walk her anywhere?"

"Aww, shucks, you're going to make me blush?"

"Blush away, my brotha, blush away."

He continued to hold her hand, and she loved the way his palm felt against hers. It was the first time she'd ever experienced a man with hands so large that hers practically disappeared. It was a good feeling, too. A wonderful feeling, actually.

~ ~ ~

The Civic Center was crowded; it seemed as if everybody had come to see this play on opening night. They were escorted to their seats in the elegant theater. Alex paused to allow Danithia to enter the row first, she sat, then he sat. His bulky frame barely fit. His shoulders touched hers and he looked extremely uncomfortable.

"Lift your arm," she said.

"Oh yeah, if I put my arm around you, that'll give me some room."

She laughed and swatted at him.

"That's not why I said lift your arm," she said, raising the arm rest to an upright position. "See."

"That's much better," he said and snuggled a little closer to her. He placed her hand palm down against his thigh. He patted it softly as if to say, your hand is safe right here. The feel of his muscular thigh beneath her slightly quivering hand, told her that he must work out, the hardness was unmistakable. She almost couldn't concentrate.

Then the play began. They watched with fascination as the two women mesmerized the audience with their stories. Having lived over a hundred years, their experiences spanned the gamut from slavery, to the tumultuous civil rights struggle of the 60s, the Black power movement of the 70s. Bessie and Saddie Delany had lived through and chronicled the Great Depression, two world wars, the struggle for and against segregation in this country, the horrible events—lynchings, hangings, and burnings of Black men and women by the hands of men who were part of the so-called secret society, the KKK. They had known and lived through countless presidencies that included Eisenhower, John F. Kennedy, and Richard Nixon. There was so much power and passion in the way they spoke about such great men as Dr. Martin Luther King, Jr., Malcolm X, the powerful and charismatic Jesse Jackson, and many, many more. With the kind of passion that echoed through the walls, off the stage, and into everyone's heart, they told their story—they had their say. And at times it was difficult to hear.

During the play, one of the Delany sisters told the story of the time she'd almost been lynched by White men, but they couldn't catch her. She ran into the woods, and hid there for hours. Danithia felt Alex flinch, and he began to tremble. She gave him a curious look and although it was

pretty dark, she saw tears running down his face. He did-
n't hide them or quickly brush them away, even when he
knew she was looking at him. He felt the emotion of these
women's experiences, and he wasn't afraid to allow himself to weep over the injustices and their obvious pain. It
was at that moment that Danithia's heart was completely
swept away. Alex Powers was a special, sensitive man—a
rare jewel—and she wanted to know more about him.

Toward the end of the play, the sisters actually prepared
a festive dinner. Danithia heard Alex's stomach growl.
She reached over to pat his tummy, then she whispered in
his ear, "Hungry, huh?"

"You heard that?" he whispered back.

"Everybody heard it."

~ ~ ~

Dinner was excellent, as well as the conversation. They
learned so much about one another, discovering similar
passions and ideologies. And with each new discovery,
their admiration for each other grew. After this first date,
they had many more ... conversations late into the night,
sometimes about nothing. And through even trivial mus-
ings they discovered nuances about one another that they
truly liked.

Meanwhile, Danithia's quest for justice for Patricia
Griffin against Comex continued. Sometimes she'd discuss
insignificant portions of the case with Alex, but for the
most part, she kept details to herself.

And she never knew he was working on it, too.

Chapter 5

"**D**anithia, this is Lyle McGregor, please come to the main conference room?"

Surprised, she uttered, "Sure, sure thing. Now?"

"Yes. Now," was his terse reply before she heard the audible click.

What the hell's going on? she wondered, as she grabbed a pen and her legal pad, then rushed down the hall.

When she entered the conference room, there were four partners there. Pat wasn't one of them. She instinctively knew something ugly was about to happen.

"Good morning, gentlemen."

"Good morning, Danithia. Please take a seat."

She knew she was on shaky ground but had no idea why. She crossed the room to sit in the chair next to Lyle, the one he was holding out for her.

She gingerly sat and folded her hands on top of the table, clasping them tight to keep them from shaking.

"Danithia, we called this impromptu meeting to advise you that it is the intention of the partners in this room to pull out of the action you have pending against Comex."

Her heart hammered heavily in her chest. She actually felt each heart beat, and her mouth went dry. Almost unable to speak she uttered a helpless, "Why?"

"We do not feel that it is in this firm's best interest to continue to pursue the matter. It is not cost effective."

"Yes," Gerald Primes timidly chimed in. "We've looked at the numbers between the cost to the firm to handle this contingency fee case, what with the enormous costs and fees already incurred, we feel that even in the unlikely event you prevail at trial, we will not recover near-ly as much as we've spent."

"I've tried my best to keep the costs down," Danithia almost pleaded, then she remembered something. "Ms. Griffin has been paying the costs anyway. I...don't... understand."

Franklin Ditz said, "We don't expect you to understand. We expect you, as a member of this firm, to simply walk away from this case, turn over your files to whomever they can get to represent them."

He said the word *they* in such a way that Danithia's skin began to crawl. Fear quickly turned to anger.

"What's the real problem here? And please don't patronize me by telling me it's money. I've worked here long and hard enough to know how much money we put out on all our contingency fee cases before we see a dime!" She looked around the table, daring anyone of them to look her in the eye. None did.

"Danithia, I know you probably think this is a . . . a race issue," Gerald stammered. "But it isn't. There are factors here that really don't concern you, and we are not at liber-ty to discuss all of them with you. It's a matter of finance. It's as simple as that"

"Does Pat agree with you? Does he, too, want to pull out of this case?" Danithia questioned.

"As I said, this is coming to you at the request of the four partners you see seated here now."

Her mind clicked while she tried to quickly assess the situation. What was going on? Why did they want out? And where was Patrick?

"With all due respect, gentlemen, I've done a lot of work on this matter. Most of my discovery is complete, and I have a solid case against Comex. I'm certain a jury will award extensive damages to the plaintiffs, and a third of that will come to the firm."

"Ms. Gilberts." Lyle smirked. "And might I ask how many cases you have tried to be able to make that boastful determination of what a jury will do?"

She stared at him and, with eyes that blazed, she answered him. "More than I can count."

He waved his hand dismissively. "I mean civil cases, not those . . . those criminal matters you used to handle."

They all snickered.

She held her head high. "Whether civil or criminal, the elements of a good attorney, an excellent trial lawyer, are the same. More than anything, we, in this room, know for a fact that it is not the innocence or guilt of a person that sets them free or gets them a positive verdict, it's the person they have chosen to be their mouth piece. And in this case, that person is me. And . . . I never lost any of my cases, even when the criminal was as guilty as the four of you sitting in this room."

Faces in unison began to turn crimson, and she knew she'd hit the mark. Now she intended to go for blood.

"If you snatch this case away from me, so help me God, I'll have this firm investigated for a number of improprieties, and I don't think you want to challenge me on my ability to do that. I've been here for quite a while and I've seen many, many things. Participated in some, in fact." Alex's accusation of "ambulance chasing" came to mind, and she cringed. He didn't know how close to the mark he came that day.

The weight of her words hung in the air like a bad case of gas. Their faces became distorted as if they smelled something rank.

Lyle spoke first, clearing his throat. "Now look here, Danithia. Don't you sit there and try to threaten us. I've chewed up and spit out better attorneys than you'll ever be!"

Gerald raised his hand in protest, an attempt to silently encourage Lyle to change his tone. "Danithia, there's no need to issue threats. Perhaps—" He looked around the room at the other partners. "Perhaps a solution would be for your clients to pay a thirty-thousand-dollar retainer for costs, and you could continue to litigate the matter."

Incredulous, she glared at him. "Sure thing, Gerald. And with all due respect, as soon as you can provide me with evidence of a retainer fee in the substantial amount you just mentioned that this firm secured from the elderly people we represented in that banking scandal, I'll gladly get my people to also provide a like retainer."

Again she had them in an uncomfortable place. They stirred in their seats as if they were systematically being pulled by a puppeteer's string.

"We'll get back to you."

"You do that, gentlemen." She rose. "I'm actually look-ing forward to having my day in court."

~ ~ ~

She returned to her office furious, heat rising to her head and burning her cheeks. If she could turn red, she'd be as bright as a beet right now. What audacity! The battle she thought she'd have to fight in court, she was seeing now had to be waged within the walls of her very own firm. And she found that ironic. Instead of supporting her, they wanted her to fail, give up, and walk away. Well, she would show them what she was made of. She wasn't brought up to be a wimp or anybody's fool. She knew what she was doing and why, and she also knew that nobody was going to stop her from achieving her goals. Nobody!

And where the hell is Pat? she seethed, wondering if he, too, was turning his back on her.

She placed a call to his secretary who said he hadn't come in today, or yesterday either. Nor had he called. Danithia's brow wrinkled. Pat rarely took off, and she had certainly never heard of him taking off without advising his secretary.

She had a hunch she could not shake. She grabbed her purse, rummaging through it for her personal phone book, found Pat's number, and dialed. No one answered. She slowly hung up the phone. She knew something was wrong. She dug further into her bag, found her keys, and headed out the door.

~ ~ ~

As was becoming her nightly ritual, she stopped at the security guard's desk to chat briefly with Alex before she headed home. But he wasn't there. The disappointment she felt surprised her. It instantly invoked feelings of despair. Funny, how something as simple as not seeing someone's face could invoke feelings like this. That was when she knew she was seriously falling for him.

Danithia chided herself for acting so foolish about not seeing Alex tonight. She had other fish to fry, other battles to wage, and most of all she needed to find and talk to Patrick. She was completely preoccupied with her own thoughts, unaware of her surroundings until movement caught her eye in the garage, by her car.

Alex stood up quickly. A startled cry escaped her lips. Then she saw the damage. All four tires on her car were flat.

"Danithia, I— I—" Alex stammered.

"You what!" she shouted. "Slashed my tires, you idiot!" Fury blinded her. "What the hell do you think you're doing!"

Raising his hands in defense as if she was about to strike him, Alex blinked rapidly.

"Hold on. Now you just wait a minute."

"No, you wait a minute! What the hell is going on here?" Danithia shouted, eyes blazing.

"I don't know. One of the tenants came to me and said a car had been vandalized. I came down here to inspect it. I didn't even know the car would be yours."

"What were you doing, sneaking around behind the car like that?"

"I wasn't sneaking around the car—"

"The hell you weren't. And to think just a few minutes ago I was actually feeling sad because I didn't see you at the desk. All the while you were down here destroying my car!"

"Danithia, calm down."

"Calm down. Don't you dare tell me to calm down. You— you—bastard!" Danithia, unable to calm herself, swung at him.

Alex caught her wrist in midair and gently held it. "Listen, Danithia. Listen!" He shook her gently. "I...did ...not...do...this!"

Danithia said nothing. She just kept staring coldly from him to the mutilated tires.

"Do you hear me?" Alex continued. "Danithia! How could you think I would do this to your car?"

She looked into his eyes and did not see maliciousness, but compassion. And realization came to her just a little too late. She knew—she sensed—that he hadn't done this horrible thing to her, but the ugly, accusatory words had already flown from her lips, and it was too late to catch or retract them. She realized that severe damage had been done to their budding, new relationship, and she regretted her quick temper and hasty, angry words.

She was about to lose her most precious, important case ever, and now she'd gone and also spoilt her friendship with Alex. It was all too much, happening too fast. She broke her own policy of never shedding tears in public, and wept at all of the day's events.

Alex took her in his arms. "Danithia, please don't . . . don't cry," he crooned, his voice soothing and understanding.

But she couldn't stop. Now that the dam was broken, the cycle had to be completed. "Alex, I—I'm."

"I know, Danithia, you didn't mean the things you said. It's okay."

His words of forgiveness, so readily given, brought on a fresh flood of tears. He held her close, allowing her to pour out her heart.

Then he took her by the hand, and she followed him without question. They entered the small security office.

"Sit down, Danithia. I'll be right back."

She numbly sat and looked around the room. There were stacks of papers in neat piles covering most of the desk. The office was organized with file folders, each labeled and stacked horizontally and vertically separated. The office was very non-committal. No personal effects. No pictures. Only a functional calendar hung on the wall. There was nothing that said anything about who occupied this space for much of the day. The exception was a crystal candy dish holding a mound of butterscotch candies.

Alex returned. He looked uncomfortable, almost as if he was afraid to approach her. He kneeled beside her and took both her hands in his.

"Danithia, I know you thought I had something to do with flattening your tires, but I didn't." He held up his hand to stop her from protesting. "I can prove I didn't do

it, and . . . I may be able to find out who actually did van-
dalize your car."

"How?"

"With this!" He reached inside his jacket and pulled
out a videotape. "This building has a security surveillance
tape that rotates throughout the parking garage and certain
corridors."

"Really!" Then her eyes grew wide with shock as she
thought about the times she had actually lifted her skirt to
adjust her slip or pantyhose when she was in the elevator
alone. "Even the elevators have surveillance?"

"No, not the elevators."

"Whew! That's good."

"Why?"

"Never mind. Just put the tape on, please. Let's see if
we can nail whoever did this."

Alex said nothing, but, continuing to kneel by her side,
gave her a long, penetrating look.

"What? Why are you still looking at me? Put the tape
in!" she demanded.

He waited a moment longer, then stood abruptly and
walked over to the television that had a video recorder
attached to it.

"As I said there's rotating surveillance, so it may or may
not have been sweeping the area when this activity was
going on. So if we don't see anything, please don't be disappointed. Okay?"

"Okay, I understand."

"And this tape is audio as well as visual, so at times it
might be a bit distracting as we hear voices, and stuff."

He inserted the tape, and they heard the whirling sound
of it being re-wound. Danithia waited patiently.

"Here goes." Alex pushed play.

For almost thirty minutes, they saw nothing of any significance, then a view of the garage, level one, came on. Level two, then level three. Danithia sat up, just on the edge of her seat. Squinting as if that would help her see better, she watched. She saw a woman in a business suit get inside a Ford Explorer. Okay. Then she heard the audible beep of an alarm being deactivated. Then the camera caught a very large man entering the small confines of a Miata.

"Now, that's what I call a tight fit," Alex said.

"Sho you right," Danithia said, using Valerie's favorite saying.

Then they heard forced air, a moment later an audible pop, more forced air escaping. Danithia's blood ran cold as she recognized that this must be what deflating and slashing tires sound like. Again they heard, but could not see the destruction. Pop. Whew. Pop. Whew. Pop. Whew. It continued like a macabre mantra. Danithia left her chair and peered at the set, trying to see what the camera did not catch.

Then the camera finally swept over the north end of the parking structure, and her car came into focus. There was nobody there.

"Damn!" she shouted in frustration and turned her back on the screen.

"Wait a minute, wait just a minute."

She turned to see the back of a man disappearing toward the stairwell. He had stringy blond hair, was of medium build, and he wore blue jeans and a non-distinct black t-shirt.

"Do you think he did it?" Danithia asked.

"Don't know." He froze the camera and stared at the distorted stilled image. His concentration on the image was such that Danithia had to speak to him twice before he heard her.

"Alex! What's the matter?"

Frowning, he looked at her.

"What a waste of time!" she exclaimed.

"Not really," Alex replied. "Somebody may have seen him. I mean, he may have left through the stairwell, but he had to come in the front door. That's another tape. I'll check it later."

"Why not check it now?"

"Because it's a much longer tape, and I've got to study it, and I can't do that right now."

"Then when can you do it?"

"Tonight. After hours. I'll check it out."

"Will you let me know what you find?"

"Of course."

"Better yet, I want to watch it with you."

"Why? You don't trust me?"

"That's beside the point," she said, waving her hand dismissively. "The point is, two eyes are better than one."

"I've got two eyes, Danithia."

"Four . . . I mean four. Oh you know what I mean. I've got to call the auto club, and maybe they can replace my tires. God," she said hands outstretched toward the heavens, "what next!"

"I don't know, but it sure looks like somebody doesn't like that pretty Lexus you've got."

"Yeah, it sure looks that way. You know, when I had my little unassuming Rabbit, nobody messed with that thing, not even when it was brand, spanking new. Damn all my friends for talking me into this darn car."

"Yeah, damn all your friends for causing you such trouble." He looked at her with a mock expression of outrage.

"You're right. It's not their fault. I'm just so . . . so tired. Today's been such an ugly day."

"Can I give you a hug? Might help lift your spirits," he said smiling, his arms opened wide.

It only took a second before she walked into his embrace, wrapped her arms around him, laying her cheek against his broad chest. She took a deep breath and exhaled.

He held her and rested his chin on the top of her head. He, too, took a deep breath and exhaled.

"Will you stop mocking me?" she said, angrily pulling away.

He gave her a startled look, "I'm not."

"Do you always have to be a comedian? Can't you ever just be human?"

"I am. I mean, I was. I mean, I wasn't mocking you. I...I took a deep breath too, that's all. I was...I was..."

"What? You were what?"

"I was smelling your hair," he said shyly. "It smells like raspberries."

"Oh." She lowered her eyes in embarrassment.

He cupped her chin and raised her face. He studied her eyes, outlined her lips with the tip of his finger, then he bent to lightly brush his lips against hers.

The moment he made the contact to touch her, she felt wonderful, electrified. She smelled butterscotch. She took another deep breath, closed her eyes, and allowed him to sweep his lips lightly across hers, back and forth, back and forth. He didn't press, he didn't prod, he just swept. It was such a wonderful, unusual sensation that she was unsure of how long—of how many times he stroked her that way, and it didn't matter. This was the most intriguing kiss she'd ever received. It was soft and warm, non-intrusive, sensual. Any moment she expected to feel the warm probing of his tongue, but he didn't go there.

Against her lips he asked, "Do you like butterscotch?"

Weakly she whispered, "Yes."

He released her then. Went over to his desk and offered the entire candy dish to her.

She watched him, noticed him trying to covertly adjust his pants, even shaking his leg slightly. She wanted to laugh.

"Should I take the whole bowl?" she queried.

"If you want."

"No, thanks." She plucked one from the top. "This will do fine. I'll see you later. Come to my office and get me when you start to survey the tape. Okay?"

"Sure." He cleared his throat, placing the jar back where it had come from. When he looked up again, all he saw was her round, firm, retreating, sashaying behind.

Long after the door to his tiny office had closed, he was still thinking about her. That kiss was not supposed to happen. He was not really supposed to get this close to her. He wasn't supposed to care. But he did. And it scared him.

~ ~ ~

By the time Danithia got back to her office, relayed to Valerie what had happened to her car and listened to her rant and rave, advising her to immediately call the police, Danithia forgot all about Pat. Valerie took her to purchase four new tires. Danithia got the auto club to put them on. She was so weary by the time the whole process was done because everyone who came into the parking structure wanted to know what happened to her car. She tired of explaining the scenario over and over again. The short answer was a simple "I don't know," but certain people—

her co-workers for instance—wanted a more in-depth explanation, which she felt compelled to give.

After her beautiful Lexus had four new tires on it, she wanted to stand there and protect it from any further vandalism, but she knew she could not do that. She resolved that if she had to get rid of this car to regain a semblance of peace, then she would do just that. No car was worth this amount of stress she reasoned.

Her day was sufficiently shot and she scrambled to catch up. It was a good thing she was going to be working late anyway. She glanced at her watch and hoped Alex wouldn't come for her for a long time.

She worked passionately. It seemed that every time she picked up where she left off with her case for Ms. Griffin against Comex, she felt empowered in a way that amazed her. She researched, she followed up by reading investigative reports, she made notes, outlined strategy, a list of deponents for deposition, and she tracked down a possible list of experts to testify at trial. She now knew who the players were behind Comex Manufacturing, and she wanted to go after them as if she had both barrels of a semiautomatic gun. Their defense was that Dr. Zimmerman acted on his own behalf, that they never authorized him to do human testing, that they did not fund his clinic, nor did they support his actions. In short, they denied all the allegations made in the Complaint. Danithia didn't believe a word of it. How could he—no, why would Dr. Zimmerman do such a thing without their knowledge? The patent for the product was not his, therefore he would never get any credit for the success of the product ... if it had been successful. What purpose did it serve for him to go forward with human testing if the product wasn't ready? Further, who funded his elaborate clinic, nestled high in the mountains, in the elite community of Boulder,

Colorado? His financial statements proved him to be economically deficient. He still could not be found, but
Danithia concentrated her efforts on Comex. If monetary
compensation was all the plaintiffs could get, then they'd
have to get it from Comex. They were jointly and several-
ly responsible for the actions of anyone in their employ,
and Dr. Zimmerman was clearly an employee. His name
appeared on Comex's financial statements as well as their
employment records. He even had a title, Director of
Marketing and Research. So why didn't they know where
he was? She added this question to her long list of additional things to have Comex clear up through document
requests or interrogatories.

She entered the library and pulled several pertinent
books from the shelves. She took her yellow legal pad and
made more notes, wrote down several cases that she felt
might be relevant and helpful to her case. She worked this
way for hours.

Glancing at her wristwatch, she noted the time to be ten
o'clock. She raised both arms and stretched, rolled her
head from side to side, unlocking the kinks that had begun
to form. She was ready to call it a night. She hoped Alex
would be coming for her soon. She started to put the vol-
umes of books back where they belonged when, suddenly,
the room went pitch black. At first she didn't panic
because she knew the building turned off the lights at a certain time every evening. Then she remembered it was only
ten. Normally, lights went out after eleven. Her heart
raced. There was a little light coming from a green exit
sign and that was all. The library was in the interior of the
building, without windows or emergency lights. There
were no telephones either, this was a place where people
came to work, and the distractions of ringing telephones
was purposely eliminated. Heart pounding, she stumbled

toward the exit sign. She knew this place like the back of her hand, but the total darkness took away some of her ability to focus clearly. Fear blocked her mind. All she heard was the swishing of her pumps against the thick carpeting. She told herself not to panic but to concentrate on getting back to her office to call security, to tell them to turn the lights back on.

~ ~ ~

Alex stepped from the elevator. Just as he reached the corridor, the place was plunged into darkness. He froze. The fine hairs along the back of his neck stood up, and he knew something was wrong. He wished he had his revolver, but he didn't. He stood still, quietly listening. He heard nothing.

Even though he was a big man, he proceeded with stealth. He crept, using the wall as a guide, grateful that his eyes had somewhat adjusted to the darkness. He thought about calling out her name, but didn't want to startle her or, if this was a dangerous situation, he didn't want to alert anyone else that he was there.

He knew these halls, knew them very well, in fact. This was one of many trips he'd made late at night to these offices, although he always had the benefit of light before. In his mind, he knew exactly where Danithia's office was. He extracted the flashlight from his waist band and headed in that direction.

He entered her office, flashed the light around, but she wasn't there. Her computer was on and, he noticed, as he rounded the desk, that her purse was still there. She's here somewhere. He hoped this thing hadn't escalated to the point that anyone had done physical harm to her. If that had happened, he would never forgive himself. Now, with rising panic, he left her office, headed toward the greenish glow coming from an exit sign.

"Danithia!" he called.

She was on the verge of hyperventilating, so unnerved was she to be caught in this building alone, in total darkness. When she heard her name, she stifled a scream.

"Alex?"

"Danithia!" Alex called again.

"Alex? Is that you?"

He flashed the light on her, saw her frightened face and his heart began to beat wildly in his chest. Running towards her, he swept her in his arms and hugged her so hard that he took her breath away.

"Babe. Are you okay?" He asked, his voice trembled.

"Alex, I was so scared. I was in the library when everything went black."

"I was so worried about you. Let's get out of here."

"Wait, I need to get my purse."

Alex took her by the hand and led the way, past three closed doors, until they entered her office. He picked up the telephone but there was no dial tone.

"The phone's dead," he said.

"Why would the phones be out?" she asked.

"I don't know. All I know is we need to get off this floor and back to the lobby. Right now!" Alex said.

Again, Alex took her by the hand. He noticed she was trembling. He stopped and embraced her, then he whispered in her ear, "Everything's going to be all right, Danithia. Do you trust me?"

"Yes, yes I do. Alex, you're scaring me."

"Don't be. Now, let's get back downstairs."

He used his flashlight and led them back to the elevators.

"Right before the lights went out I was thinking about you, wondering when you were going to come get me."

He hadn't really heard her. He was busy watching the elevator numbers as they descended to the lobby. Twenty-one floors to go. Suddenly, the number stayed illuminated on the tenth floor.

"Uh oh."

"What?"

"I think we're stuck. Damn!" Alex said, as he pushed the lobby button several times, then attempted to open the call box. Then, the lights went out again. He fumbled with his keys, knowing that one of them would manually operate the elevator. He handed the flashlight to Danithia while he looked for it. The key was gone.

"Oh, shit," he mumbled.

"Oh my God, not only are we stuck, but it's so damn dark! This has got to be the worst day of my life!" Danithia said, slapping her palm against her forehead.

Alex pulled and punched the call box in frustration.

"Damn thing won't open. There's a phone in here, but what good does that do us if we can't get to it!"

He willed himself to calm down. If he panicked, she'd panic. Not a good combination.

"Okay, Danithia, this is what we're going to do. Don't be alarmed, we're going to get out of here. Of course, that would be so much easier if I hadn't left my walkie-talkie downstairs with Stephen."

"Who's Stephen?" she asked.

"The other security officer. I hope he notices before too much longer that we're stuck. If he's paying attention, the monitors will show the elevator has stopped on ten."

They were trapped, at least for the time being, inside the narrow confines of the elevator. He noticed that she was very quiet, except her breathing had become harsh and rapid.

"Danithia, are you okay?"

"I...I sometimes suffer...panic attacks in small spaces. It hasn't happened...in such a long time...not since...I was a child. I thought I was over it."

"Okay, okay," he said soothingly, "You're okay. Do you hear me, babe? You're with me and I won't let anything happen to you."

He held her in his arms, hoping that his touch would calm her fears. Finally, he felt her body begin to relax, and her breathing returned to normal. Her perfume seemed to surround him. It swirled about his head and filled the interior of his nostrils. He so badly wanted to inhale deeply, let the aroma of whatever perfume she was wearing, coupled with her own natural scent, to provide him with sensual delight. This was not the time. He tried to repress those feelings.

"Alex, I'm okay now," she whispered.

Her voice in a whisper was even more sensual to him than ever before and he was beginning to feel like he was fighting a losing battle with himself. He wanted to control his emotions, but he also desperately wanted to let them go. He wanted the elevator to start to move. But he wanted to stay right where he was too, with her wrapped tightly in his protective embrace. He wanted the lights back on, but he also wanted to close his eyes and taste her.

"Alex?" she said again, her hand lightly pressed against his chest.

She felt his breath, hot and moist against her face, it was tinged with the now familiar scent of butterscotch. With a sudden vivid memory, she recalled his version of a kiss, the one he'd given her earlier today and a feeling of desire swept through her like the warmth of a Colorado summer breeze.

"Alex?"

"What?"

"What's going to happen? What's really going on?"

He heard the panic that was beginning to rise again in her voice. With no warning, no thought at all, he cradled each side of her face with his palms.

Then he kissed her. His lips lightly brushed hers, and she tasted sweet. She was soft, as soft as cotton candy. And like cotton candy that instantly melts, disappearing like magic on your tongue, leaving the wonder and joy of decadent pleasure behind, she left a trail of magic wonder upon every cell, every millimeter of the skin she touched.

He pulled away trying to peer into the face of an angel. He could barely make out her features. He ran his thumb over her lips—now wet—glistening with moisture he put there, and at that very moment he could easily devour her, savor every inch of her in slow, deliberate morsels. He claimed her lips again, applying just enough pressure to force them open. He inwardly rejoiced when she willingly acquiesced. He gently licked the parameters of her lips, then, as soft as a whisper, slipped his tongue inside the warm, sensual contours, probed her tongue, suckled it tenderly. He swept every inch of her mouth, getting lost, falling deeper, deeper into heaven . . . and for one split second, he was reduced to a helpless man, as he finally realized he could surrender. And surrender he did to love.

Danithia wrapped her arms more tightly around him. She felt lost and found, all at the same time. How can that be, she wondered. But it was true. In his embrace, she felt so very, very safe and . . . loved. His kiss sent her back in time, a time when she hungered for tenderness, for a love to call her own. Tumbled emotions swept through her. She thought it might be futile to pursue a relationship with him. The differences in their respective lives, their careers, their life choices, seemed like obstacles neither one of them could overcome. It was funny, but even though these thoughts were going through her head—even with her eyes closed—she could see his face, the hard lines that were etched at the corners of his mouth, evidence of a man who is no stranger to smiling—to laughter. Her heart leapt when she realized that her mind's eye could see so many details about him that, until now, she hadn't known she'd noticed.

She wanted to speak but couldn't. Her extensive vocabulary failed her, for there were no words to adequately explain the way she felt. Then she realized she didn't have to talk. There was no need to articulate.

She returned his kiss with urgent passion—passion stored up from at least a thousand sleepless nights. With everything filling the depths of her soul, she too surrendered.

And, really, no words were necessary.

~ ~ ~

"Alex?"

"Um-hmm."

"We're moving again."

"What?" he said. His eyes popped open and he was happy to see the nine, eight, seven, six, five, four, until the doors opened on the first floor to blinding brilliance. Blinking, and a bit disoriented, they stepped out of the elevator.

As Alex approached the front desk console, he frowned. Anytime an elevator failed to operate correctly, a warning light would flash on the console and security would be immediately notified that there was a malfunction. But there was no such evidence. And there was no Stephen.

"What's wrong?" Danithia asked, noticing the worry lines that etched his brow.

For a moment he said nothing, but punched buttons on the computer. Just as he had suspected, someone had turned elevator number four off, then, later, turned it back on. As a safety precaution this was something they had the ability to do, but it was done only at the request or instruction of the building supervisor. And if ever this procedure was implemented, for obvious reasons, it was always documented. A sense of urgency came over him. Where was Stephen?

"Alex?"

He looked at her then, making a hasty decision not to tell her that they had been deliberately trapped in the elevator. Until he knew why, he wasn't going to worry her. "Look, I think in light of what's happened tonight, we should just call it a night. I promise to look at the tape tomorrow and, if you like, we can do it together."

"Alex, what aren't you telling me?"

"What makes you think I'm not telling you something?"

"How about the fact that you've got about five worry lines etched in your forehead right now, not to mention it sure looks like you're suppressing a scowl."

"You don't know me well enough to be able to read my face."

"That's what you think. But, for now, I'll play the game your way, but I want you to remember two things, okay?"

"What?"

"One, I was in that elevator too, so if there's something going on that I need to know about, you should feel obligated to tell me. And two, only because I trust you, will I allow you to evade answering my questions right now."

He stared at her and grappled with himself about telling her. "Okay. All I'm going to say is this. If you really do trust me, trust that I'm looking out for you, and if and when

I know something that I can share with you, then I will. Okay?"

"Fair enough."

He looked over Danithia's shoulder at the lobby door. "There's Stephen."

They both noticed Stephen as he blew a trail of smoke before entering the building.

Alex watched him suspiciously. According to the building management rules, the front lobby was never to be left unattended, not even for a smoke break. So, why had Stephen broken the rules?

"Danithia, if you can wait just a few more minutes, I'll leave with you, my eleven o'clock relief should be here any minute."

"I'm really tired, Alex. I just want to go home now."

Stephen watched them for a minute, then said, "Alex, Bart's here. You can leave if you want to."

"Great!" Alex said with forced enthusiasm. "Just let me grab my jacket and I'll see you home."

"Alex," she protested. "You don't have to do that."

"Yes, I do. Remember, you trust me."

"With my life," she replied, looking him in the eye.

He left her then, and she chatted briefly with Stephen. Alex soon returned, and he seemed even more distracted.

"What is it, Alex?"

He looked up at her startled, like he was unsure of what exactly it was he wanted to say. "The tape's gone."

"What do you mean it's gone? What happened to it?"

"I left it sitting on my desk when I went upstairs to get you, and now it's gone."

"Something very strange is going on here. Somebody's trying to keep us away from finding out who's messing with my car. Who would do such a thing, Alex? Who would take the tape?"

Alex hesitated, then said, "Let me check again. Maybe I put it somewhere else. I'll be right back."

He briskly walked away, and she watched him until he disappeared. Her mind went into overdrive. Everything that had been happening was not a coincidence. She even suspected that the damage to her car was part of some sort of elaborate scheme. To do what? she wondered. Scare me? Then she rapidly went through the last few weeks in her mind and analyzed what was going on that would cause someone to want to scare her away from something. What could that something be? The only thing she knew was different was the Comex case and while that case was intriguing, was it enough to cause someone to want to harm her?

Alex returned. "It's not there. I checked everywhere."

"Alex, I'm so upset right now, all I want to do is go home."

"Sure."

"Goodnight, Stephen," Alex said, "Have a good one. And," he paused, "tomorrow, you and I are going to talk about some things that happened tonight."

Alex walked away not giving Stephen a chance to respond.

~ ~ ~

Alex followed her home and was enough of a gentlemen to see her to her door, deposit a light kiss upon her cheek, then retreated.

She slowly undressed and got into bed, her mind rapidly jumping from one scenario to another. She had almost fallen asleep when, suddenly, she sat straight up in bed.

"Pat! I forgot to go see about Pat."

She glanced at the clock, and it was entirely too late to call him. But she'd phone first thing in the morning.

Chapter 6

Danithia finished her cup of coffee with a hot bowl of oatmeal and toast, rinsed her dishes and put them in the dishwasher. This morning she was on a mission. It was imperative that she try to see Pat today, and she wanted to do so without further delay. As if unseen hands were propelling her forward, there was nothing that would stop her from finding out where he was. What was his position on her continuing to work on the Comex matter? Soon, there would be no further need to wonder for she intended to ask him herself.

Upon entering her garage she was instantly propelled back to the events of yesterday. Again, she worried about what was going on and why someone kept vandalizing her car. Preoccupied, she backed the car out and started to drive away before she remembered to use the remote and close the garage door. She did not look back. Therefore, she did not see the young White man with a stringy ponytail, blue jeans, and a non-distinct black t-shirt slipping into her garage.

~ ~ ~

Danithia took the congested interstate 70 to Green Valley Ranch and the home of Patrick O'Leary. She had been there once before, he had invited all the associates at the firm for a barbecue. Everyone was instructed to wear cowboy hats and boots, handkerchiefs, and a tall Stetson, if possible. She had to go to a costume shop to get that kind of outfit. But it was fun. They line danced and whooped and hollered, gorged themselves on barbecue ribs, chicken, and roast beef, potato salad and sweet baked beans, corn on the cob, and peach cobbler.

Pat had a huge barrel full of some kind of liquor concoction and invited them to simply dip in the ladle and fill their silver tin cups. She learned how to square dance and attempted to ride a mechanical horse. But the highlight of the evening was when members of the Black cowboys showed up and put on a mini performance for them. She recalled how pleasantly surprised she was to see about a half dozen Black men appear, all dressed up in cowboy gear. They gathered the crowd and put on a performance that she would never forget. She met each one of them and had her hand kissed repeatedly as they bowed to her, calling her ma'am, and telling her how much they liked what she wore. She was more than flattered. She was also amazed that Patrick knew them by name, and they seemed to be good friends. Pat was full of surprises, and his love for people of color was indeed genuine.

She arrived at his expansive ranch-style home, nestled on thirty acres of beautiful land, but she did not see his automobile. She really hadn't expected to, since he had a three-car garage, where he kept his cars—his toys, as he called them.

She parked her car and walked up the circular driveway to ring the doorbell. She waited, but he did not answer. She called out his name. Still no answer. She flipped open her cell phone and dialed the office. He was not in. She hung up, then dialed his home number. She could hear the shrill ringing on the south side of the house. She stood there a minute longer, then proceeded along the stone path around the house until she heard the phone loud and clear behind a large window. She flipped the phone closed and peered inside. She could see Pat. He was lying on his bed, his head hanging awkwardly over the side. She called out his name, but he did not answer. She knocked on the window, then she thought she saw a slight movement of his head.

"Pat!" she screamed. "Are you all right?"

Nothing.

"Pat! Is something wrong?" She began to feel panic rise within her. "Pat!" she shouted. "I'm going to break the window if you don't answer me. Please answer me!"

She mumbled to herself, "God, I don't want to do this." But she knew she had to.

Snatching up a large sharp-edged stone, she hurled it at the window and jumped back as fragments of glass exploded everywhere. Then she thought about Pat, fearful that she might have hurt him. He had not budged. Concern propelled her forward. With her jacket wrapped around her arm, she swept away the remaining shards of glass and hoisted herself over the windowsill.

She rushed to the bed and leaned over him. His eyes were open and he blinked. His breathing seemed very shallow.

"Pat!"

His eyes closed and opened again.

"What's wrong? Can't you move?"

He blinked again. She noticed that his cordless telephone was right at his fingertip, but his hand was curiously curled in a twisted way. One side of his face drooped and dry spittle had formed in the corners of his mouth.

"Oh my goodness, have you had a stroke or something!" she cried. "It's okay, Pat, I'm here. I'm gonna get you some help."

She grabbed his phone and dialed the operator and gave swift instructions for paramedics to come right away.

She rubbed his hand and tried to sit him up straight. He was extremely heavy, heavier than she thought he'd be.

While she struggled with him, he watched her. Then she saw a tear slip down his cheek. It was all she could do not to start to cry herself. Instead she talked to him, smoothed his night clothes, wiped away his tears.

"I knew something was wrong. I knew it! How long you been like this? Huh? We haven't seen you at work in two days, that long Pat—that long?" she asked, incredulous that he could possibly have been in this state, alone, for two days.

She knew he couldn't speak to her, so she simply kept talking and patting and soothing him while they waited for help to arrive. "What can I do?" she asked him. "God, I've never been in a situation like this before, Pat, what do I do?"

She gently squeezed his hand. "I'm sorry, I'm sorry, I know you can't answer me. Maybe I'll call the operator again, surely there must be something I could be doing."

Then she heard the wail of the approaching ambulance. Gently, she laid Pat against the headboard, then ran toward the front of the house and fumbled with the locks until finally she opened the door.

"He's in here."

Two large men followed closely on her heels, all the while she talked.

"I just found him. Don't know how long he's been like this."

"What happened here?" one of the paramedics asked her when he saw the glass everywhere.

"Had to break the window to get in. Don't mind that, take care of him!"

They rushed over to Pat, one on each side of him. One held his wrist, searching for a pulse, while the other put a stethoscope to his chest.

"His breathing's shallow. I suspect he's been in and out of consciousness."

"Pupils unequal."

"Paralysis evident on left side."

"Skin clammy; temperature subnormal."

Danithia watched and heard the two paramedics communicate Pat's condition to one another. She was frozen for a time, it seemed she was outside of herself, like someone else looking in. Then, when they started to remove his shirt and Pat's limp body fell forward, but his eyes were open, and spittle trickled from his mouth, she couldn't take it anymore. She silently left the room.

She heard the paramedics' voices, but her mind had shut down, no longer could she understand their meaning, except when they said something about suspecting a hemorrhage in the brain. She did not want to hear any more. She wandered over to the window and watched as a fire truck arrived and more people came on the scene. She pointed to the bedroom. "He's in there."

A female police officer came over to her and took her hand. "Are you okay?" she asked, her face and voice full of compassion.

"No...I mean yes...no," Danithia whispered as her head fell forward and rested on the officer's shoulder. She finally released her tears, and she felt as if she crashed...as if everything problematic in the entire world now rested upon her shoulders. She hiccuped and sobbed and wailed in anguish. Her friend, her confidante, her one ally at the firm was suffering terribly, and she didn't know if he'd ever again be the same.

~ ~ ~

Danithia rode in the ambulance with Pat, holding his hand and stroking it, uttering words of assurance to him, while the paramedics monitored him closely. It was a lengthy ride to Aurora Presbyterian Hospital, and Danithia was very much aware of Pat's silent, frustrated stare. After a while, she started talking—as if compelled—about the office.

"Things have been kind of crazy at work, Lyle and some other partners wanting me off the Comex case." She saw Pat's eyebrow lift. "Yep, they seem to be worried about money and how much we're spending on this case. I don't believe them though, Pat. Something else is going on." She sighed, then continued, "I needed you. That's why I came out today, I wanted to talk to you. I never expected to find ..." Her voice trailed off; she didn't want to complete her thought.

"The first chance I get, I'm gonna have a little talk with God," she said, noticing his eyebrow rise again. "I've got to know why bad things happen to good people—good people like you, Pat. 'Cause frankly, I don't get it."

"God, has little to do with things like this, ma'am," the paramedic said. "I'm a firm believer that a man his age, whose blood pressure shoots up high enough to cause a stroke, well, sometimes it happens because of his lifestyle, his choices. Is he a heavy drinker?"

She thought about how blasted Patrick had wanted everybody to get at his party, insisting they keep their tin cups full, and she remembered that he was pretty drunk himself.

The paramedic continued to talk as he again placed a blood pressure cup on Pat's arm. "Looks to me like he lives the good life, nice house, plenty of eat, drink, and be merry, I suspect. And when you live like that, sooner or later you've got to pay the piper."

Danithia listened to this paramedic whose name tag said he was "Bob". She heard him spew words, acting as if he knew Pat. He didn't know anything about Pat or his lifestyle, and she resented the implications he made about the kind of man Patrick was. She was too drained to utter a response. She just looked from him back to Pat and continued to hold her old mentor's hand.

She spent the entire morning at the hospital. Between numerous telephone calls to the office, informing them of what had happened, she managed to speak to Lyle, and she found it was easier than she thought to be cordial to him. She realized she could ill afford to hold on to resentment. Lyle had a job to do, and so did she. Somehow they would have to find a way to work together, to put aside their differences. They both cared a lot about Patrick, and that was where they let their conversation lie—with Patrick.

She called Alex, knowing today was his day off. He answered on the first ring.

"Hi!"

"Hello yourself. What's going on, pretty lady?"

"More than you could imagine."

"Try me."

"I'm at Aurora Pres."

"The hospital?" he said, his voice rising.

"Yep."

"What's wrong? Why are you there?"

"Remember my friend Patrick? I told you about him."

"Vaguely."

"I found him this morning. He had a stroke."

"Found him where?"

"At his home."

"This morning?" Alex repeated.

"He hadn't been seen or heard from in the last two days. Because of the things happening at work I wanted to talk to him, so I went to his house. I found him lying— almost catatonic—" She couldn't finish her sentence as the vivid replay of finding him sent her into an emotional collapse.

"I'm sorry to hear about your friend. Will he be all right?"

"I hope so. I don't know yet."

"Is anybody there with you?"

"Nope," she sighed.

"I'm on my way."

"Alex, you don't have to do that. I'm a big girl, I can handle this."

"And I'm a big boy, capable of making my own decisions, and right now I've decided that I need to be there with you. Okay?"

She smiled and felt touched by this concern.

"I'm on the fourth floor in the ICU waiting room."

"Do you need anything?"

"A hug would be nice."

"Don't you worry, I've got plenty of those for you."

~ ~ ~

Shortly after speaking to Alex, Patrick's parents arrived. They were very concerned about him and were even more grateful to her for finding him. With their arrival, she felt pushed out of the way, no longer needed. She anxiously waited for Alex. She hoped he wouldn't mind taking her to see Ms. Griffin, since she had to leave her car at Pat's house, and her appointment with Ms. Griffin was in a couple of hours. She'd need him to either take her to get her car or take her to Cherry Creek. He'd drive her in either case. For now, she wanted only to sit in his car, allow him to make her laugh, and temporarily forget the awful beginning of this day.

She leaned her head against the cold windowpane and stared out at the beginning of tiny snow flurries. She loved the first snow. It was hazardous to drive in, but she loved the way the first snow coated the city and made everything appear to be clean, the air crisp with no traces of pollution. Every year she eagerly anticipated the first snow fall, and like a child she'd run outside in coat, hat, gloves, and boots and she'd stand there, arms opened wide, head back, and she'd close her eyes and let the cold flakes drop on her face. It was a form of spiritual cleansing for her. Nobody understood it, not even her, but she did it anyway. She gloried at the God who made such a thing as snow possible, each tiny flake having its own unique pattern. And the same snowflakes could turn a city into a disaster area, or blanket it with a smooth coating of the whitest white you'd ever see. At that moment she worshiped Him in her own special way, giving all reverence and allegiance to Him. As she watched another flake briefly cling to the glass, then slowly disappear, she wondered if today she'd get to praise Him in her own unique way.

~ ~ ~

Alex saw her standing with her forehead against the glass, and he felt his heart go out to her. She was a very special lady, and he hated like hell that all these horrible things were happening to her all because she took the Comex case. He hoped he could continue to watch over her, but things were getting a bit more dangerous. He wished for a way to tell her, but knew that he could not. Would she hate him once she found out his role in all of this? he wondered.

"Danithia?"

She turned around, slowly, and with a smile on her face she opened her arms for him, and he stepped into her embrace.

"I thought I was supposed to be giving you a hug?" he said laughing.

"You are," she replied. "I just initiated it."

They held each other for a long while. She seemed to be gathering strength from him, stroking his arms, rubbing his broad shoulders and back, and never letting her grip on him loosen.

"Umm, you feel good," he mumbled into her neck.

"So do you." She sighed. "Thank you for coming." She extracted her body from his but still continued to hold him lightly. "I've got a favor to ask of you?"

"What?"

"I have an appointment today at three with one of my clients who lives in Cherry Creek, and I left my car at Patrick's house. Could you take me either to get my car or to Cherry Creek? I could use the company and maybe, after I'm through, I could treat you to dinner."

"I'll treat you to dinner, and I'd be happy to take you anywhere you want to go."

"Anywhere?" she said, raising an eyebrow.

"Anywhere. In fact, if you like, the next stop could be the moon."

"The moon! Boy, you're pretty confident. I guess that's one of the things I like about you."

He ran his fingertip across her lips and stroked her jawbone, then he asked in a throaty voice. "Danithia, would you let me take you there?"

"Take me where?"

"To a place where the stars shine so bright you have to keep your eyes closed. A place where the heat of passion will build, starting at the bottom of your feet, rising to the very tips of the hair on your head. A place where you'll find yourself praising God, calling out his name over and over and over again."

"Stop," she said, her breathing coming faster as she visualized being in such a place with him.

"Again, I ask you, can I take you there?"

She nodded yes as she searched his face, looking for signs of mistrust, of abuse, of doggishness, and saw none. She knew he wanted to make love to her, to take her to the moon so to speak. And she wanted to take him there, too.

~ ~ ~

During the drive, Alex expressed a great deal of concern about her friend Patrick, and he praised her for her quick actions. If it weren't for her, no telling when Pat would have been found. She shuddered at the thought that Pat might have died—all alone—in his bed. They talked about death and its inevitability. Alex said he would not want to die alone, with lots of unfinished business left behind.

"Unfinished business, like what?" she asked.

"Like making and raising babies, having a family to work hard for and to cherish."

"You want children?" she asked him.

"Yes, one day I'd like to have at least three of them."

"Fatherhood's a huge responsibility. Can you handle it?"

"With you by my side, I think I could."

She looked at his profile with a bit of shock and amusement. What in the world made him think she wanted children? Her career was her child, and she didn't think she could do much more than that but before she could express her thoughts to him about motherhood, they were approaching the tricky intersection that led to Ms. Griffin's mansion. So, instead, she concentrated on the road and giving him directions.

"Do you want to come in?" she asked.

"No, this is business. I'll just sit here, listen to some music, and wait for you."

"Are you sure? It's starting to snow, it's going to get cold."

"I have a heater. Go ahead now, handle your business, I'll be fine. Go on!" he urged.

As soon as she got to the front door, it was open and Geraldine welcomed her.

"How you doin', baby?"

"Just fine, Geraldine, just fine. How about you?"

"Oh, chil', I've got my aches and pains, but I's alive. So, if the good Lord goin' to bless me with 'nother day, then I ain't 'bout to complain."

Danithia looked at the aging body of Geraldine and impulsively gave her hug. Sudden visions of Patrick came to her mind, sloped, his eyes glazed, his face contorted, and she hoped no harm would ever come to this woman, whose simple yet warm ways made Danithia feel so good—so accepted.

"Chil', you all right?" Geraldine asked.

"I'm fine, really I am. I just wanted to give you a hug and tell you how special I think you are."

Just then the black-cloaked form of Patricia Griffin stood on the staircase.

"Hello, Danithia."

"Hi, Patricia. Are you ready to go over your deposition testimony?"

"Yes, let's get started."

Danithia looked at Geraldine and whispered, "You take care of yourself, okay?"

"Yes, ma'am, I'll sho do that." Then Geraldine walked away, while Danithia and Patricia proceeded to the library.

"How are you doing today, Patricia?"

"Every day brings its own anxieties and joys. Today is one of joy, for I have you visiting."

"Thank you."

"I want to thank you for coming here instead of making me come to your office. I'm still not quite ready for public appearances."

"I understand."

"Have a seat."

"Thank you. Now, let's get down to business. Today I'm going to go over what a deposition is, brief you on the kinds of questions I think they might ask, and give you instructions on the proper way to answer. Okay?"

"Yes."

"When you are deposed you will be asked a series of questions, some of which I can gage and warn you about, some I obviously can't. If at any time during your deposition you are asked any question I find objectionable, or unnecessary, I will advise you not to answer, and even if you feel compelled to answer anyway, don't."

"Okay, I understand."

"Also, be very careful of what it is you do say and how you say it. Everything will be recorded. There may even be a videographer there."

"They'll not only be taping my voice, but also my person?"

"Yes, probably."

Patricia thought about this and didn't like it at all. "Can we ask them not to videotape me?"

"I can request no videographer if you're uncomfortable with that."

"Let's just say I'm not ready to be displayed on TV"

"It won't be on TV, but I understand what you're saying. I'll see what I can do about that."

"Will they . . ." Patricia's voice trailed off. She took a deep breath. "Will they ask me to take off my cloak?"

Danithia had known this question was coming, and she was prepared.

"They may ask you to, but you do so only if you feel comfortable. Your physical injuries are going to be analyzed and discussed in depositions with our experts, every detail of your appearance will be thoroughly outlined at another arena—and they know that—making it unnecessary for you to reveal yourself, if you don't want to.

"This will be a pretty in-depth question and answer session, which, I suspect, will take at least two days. Not only do I not want you to become stressed or fatigued, I don't want you to be uncomfortable either. As far as I'm concerned, the defendants have caused you enough pain and suffering. I won't allow them to put you through any more than is legally required."

Patricia got up and wandered around the room, her cloak softly swishing as she walked. For a while she said nothing. Then she stopped at the window and stared out, gazing at the beginning of dusk.

"Danithia, there's someone sitting in my driveway," she said with alarm.

"He's with me. It's okay."

"Why didn't you ask him to come in? Are you ashamed of me, too?"

Danithia rose from her seat and gently turned Patricia around.

"I am not ashamed of you, never have been. I did ask Alex to come in, but he declined."

Patricia stared into Danithia's eyes, searching for pity, but saw none.

"I'm sorry, I guess I'm a little paranoid these days."

"Paranoid? Why?"

"I feel like someone's been watching me—watching the house, I can't really define it, it's just something I feel, perhaps it's only my guilty conscience."

"You have nothing to feel guilty about, Patricia. In this scenario you are the victim. Someone baited you into trying a product that wasn't safe and it's their fault, not yours, that you were injured. That's what we'll show and prove not only in your deposition but also in court, if it goes that far."

"I'll show them what they've done to me if I must," Patricia said, her voice trembling.

"We'll see if that's necessary. Right now, let's go over some questions that I think they might ask. Okay? Come, let's sit back down."

She led Patricia to the sofa with her arm cradling her shoulders. She had to find a way to let Patricia know that she didn't despise her or feel ashamed of her, but how could she convince her?

They discussed the many avenues of questioning, from mild to harsh, from accusatory to feigned acquiescence. She advised her about the intricacies of tone of voice, eye contact, and gestures.

"It's really getting warm in here, don't you think?" Patricia asked Danithia.

"Actually, I'm fine," she replied, then she thought of something. "But if you're hot, take off your cloak. It looks mighty uncomfortable to me."

There was silence for what seemed like a very long time. The two women stared at each other, the suggestion hanging in the air.

"Are you sure you don't mind?" Patricia asked.

"Of course not. This is your home, and I am your guest. And . . . I'm also your friend. Please take it off. I'd like nothing more than to talk with you face-to-face."

Patricia started to cry.

"Patricia," Danithia said soothingly, "if you don't begin to forgive yourself, the healing will not start. And I'm talking about healing your mind, your heart, your soul, as well as your face and body." She continued, "There is a very strong mind/body connection, and God made us with the ability to heal ourselves—our various wounds—and if you want to start believing that you are okay again and that you are going to be whole again, it may have to start right now—today—with you doing a simple but courageous act. Take off your cloak, Patricia."

She watched for what seemed like an eternity. The room was silent except for their breathing and the tick-tock of the grandfather clock. Then Patricia took off the cloak. Her eyes were bright, brimming with tears, and her smile was genuine as she whispered a fond, "Thank you."

They continued to talk, and they laughed, and they shared stories. After about two hours, Danithia rose. They hugged each other warmly, filled with a sense of alliance and . . . friendship.

~ ~ ~

Alex had fallen asleep. A jazz station played softly, and Danithia heard the distinctive tones of a saxophone as she slipped inside the warm car.

"Wake up Alex."

"I'm not sleeping," he mumbled, "just checking my eyelids for holes."

"Yeah, right!" she said, laughing. "Do holes also come with drool?"

"I'm not drooling." He quickly swiped at the corners of his mouth. "How'd it go?"

"Fine. Actually, excellent. We've finally become friends, and together we're going to get these guys!"

"I believe you will," he said with a confident smile.

"It's starting to snow." She beamed.

"Yeah, and I hope we get out to your place before it turns into a nasty blizzard."

"You forgot we need to get my car."

"And dinner," he said.

"And dinner." Again, she smiled.

"What do you want to do first, eat or drive out to Green Valley Ranch?"

She said, "How about if we stop by my house, and I'll grill some salmon, make a tossed salad, and heat up some garlic bread."

"Sounds good to me. You sure you don't want to go out?"

"I'm sure. I'd love to cook for you."

"Really!" He glanced at her smiling face. "Why?"

"Just cause, that's all."

"You ain't trying to hook me, is you, woman?"

"No, but I'd happily give you some English lessons."

"Ain't nuttin' wrong wit my Eng-i-leesh."

She laughed and said, "Sho you right!"

"Now, look who's talking!"

~ ~ ~

Danithia fished the house keys from her purse, unlocked, and stepped inside with Alex close on her heels. She flipped on the nearest light switch and almost stumbled over her television sitting on the floor with the cord neatly wrapped around it.

"What the hell?" she said.

Then she looked around her normally immaculate living room and found everything in a total disarray.

"Oh, oh baby, looks like you've been robbed," Alex said. "Stay right here, while I check to make sure nobody's still here."

She looked around the room more frightened than ever. This can't be real, she thought. Then, as if in a dream she walked into her bedroom completely ignoring Alex's advice to stay put. She gasped. Her fur coat and several dresses were laid out on her bed in bundles, as if to be carried away. All the dresser drawers were open, the contents spilling across the lacquer top and onto the floor. Perfume bottles were turned over, and the room reeked of Obsession, Eternity, White Diamonds, and more. She sneezed. She was frozen in place, mesmerized by the destruction of her private space—her home.

A floor board creaked when Alex joined her, and she jumped.

"They pretty much trashed the kitchen. I don't think you want to see it," he said, cradling her from behind as he peered over her shoulder at the mayhem in the bedroom.

"Why, Alex? Why?" she uttered helplessly over and over again.

"I don't know, Danithia," he said. But he did know, and things were escalating, quickly getting out of hand. "We need to call the police."

She said nothing, just walked over to her fur coat and stroked it, finding little comfort in its softness. She was glad it was still there.

"I bought this coat on a whim," she told him as she continued to caress it.

"It's beautiful."

"Isn't it," she said, her voice trailing off, and she again surveyed the room.

"Oh my God, I forgot about Tanya!" She ran from the room, Alex close behind her.

The patio door was ajar, and that sight sent chills running through her body. Tanya would have been standing there, desperately trying to get in if she were okay. Danithia silently prayed, "Please God, please don't let anything happen to her." She gripped the handle and yanked the sliding glass door open so hard, it smacked into the other side and quickly sprang back almost hitting her. She froze. Tanya was lying very still in the middle of the yard.

"Tanya, come here girl! Tanya!" she yelled, smacking her thigh and making kissing noises.

Silence. Danithia didn't approach her, for she knew she had to be dead. Everyday since she'd had her, the greetings at night had always been enthusiastic and gleeful. But today, Tanya didn't budge.

"Oh, Alex," she cried, a look of horror upon her face.

"Damn baby, not the dog." He hurried around her and cautiously approached the dog. If she was only injured, she might strike out at him. But there was no life in her. A small pool of blood had formed near her head. Her mouth and eyes were open. A small piece of black cloth clung to her teeth. Alex carefully extracted it and upon inspection noted blood and some tissue.

"Well who ever killed her got bitten too."

"How do you know?" Danithia asked. Still in shock, she hadn't moved.

"There's a piece of cloth in her mouth. It's got blood on it."

"Could it be Tanya's blood?"

"It could be, but I don't think so." He saw the blood congealing around the dog's head. "Danithia, do you have an old blanket I could cover her with?"

"Yeah, I'll be right back."

Alex stood and shook his head, put his hands in his pocket, and surveyed the yard. He wandered around, looking for evidence of where the robber might have come in or out. He saw a splash of blood on the fence, pulled himself up, and peeked over. Several items that must have come from Danithia's house were lying there, the snow starting to cover them. He started to jump the fence, then thought better of it. Let the police handle it. Perhaps they'd find some useable fingerprints. He knelt by the dog again. He was tempted to turn her over, see how badly her head had been hit, but he didn't want Danithia to come back and see something she couldn't handle. Where was she? He glanced at his watch for no particular reason, except it seemed like she was taking way too long to get a blanket. A chill raced up his spine. He got up and ran.

He found her huddled in a corner, weeping as if she'd just lost her best friend. And she had. Her head was down, and muffled sobs echoed through the hallway. She had a blanket in her hand; it covered her face. He watched her for a moment as great sobs racked her body, her shoulders jerking and the sight of her broke his heart.

"Oh baby, I'm so sorry."

He knelt beside her and gathered her in his arms. He didn't try to make her stop, just sat with her and let her cry—mourn her loss, and whenever she got through, he'd be there, waiting.

"Alex, who's trying to scare me?" she asked, her voice small, timid, weak, almost helpless.

"I don't know, babe, I don't know."

She swiped at her face, smearing mascara across her cheek. He took a corner of the blanket and tried to wipe it away. He saw her staring at him. He felt uncomfortable, so he looked away.

She continued to watch him, then she surprised him and said, "Why do you look guilty?"

He raised his head to face her and almost told her the truth. But his sense of duty stopped him.

"I feel badly for you. That's not guilt you see on my face. Besides, I would never hurt you in this way. Danithia, I thought...Danithia, I thought you trusted me."

She looked at him with sorrowful eyes. "I do."

"Then why do you say stuff like that to me, if you trust me?"

"It was just an observation, not an accusation."

"That's legal talk, Danithia," he said, frustrated. "Talk to me like you would to a trusted friend, okay?"

"Alex," she said, pushing him away as she stood. "Let's not do this now. I need to call the police." She broke free from his hurtful eyes and started for the telephone. Looking back at him, she tossed the blanket. He caught it with one hand in mid-air, but she was not impressed. She realized at that moment that she could no longer afford to trust him or anybody else. She felt like she was utterly alone—and helpless.

~ ~ ~

After the police left, she and Alex stared at each other.

"Danithia, I'd feel so much better if you'd come home with me. Don't spend the night here, it might be dangerous."

She looked up at him and an army of emotions marched through her. She did not want to stay in her own house, nor did she want to go to her parents' home and worry them. She considered calling her secretary, Valerie, but thought better of that, too.

"Come on, Danithia, I won't bite. Please do this for me. I can't leave you here by yourself."

Suddenly she felt so tired, she fought the urge to just lie down in the middle of the floor and go to sleep. She knew this feeling was a direct result of stress, pressing down on her, making her feel overly fatigued. And right on the heels of stress came fear. For her, it was a lethal combination.

"All right Alex. I'll go to your place. Let me get some things."

He nodded his head in agreement. Once she left the room, he began to pick things up, he righted a lamp, returned the television to its proper place. Whoever had robbed her got her VCR, and he made a mental note to buy her one for Christmas. She told the police she had a modest stereo, and it too was gone.

He straightened the pictures on the walls, stood up portraits that had been knocked over, searched for her vacuum cleaner and started to vacuum up the remnants of dirt and green leaves from disjointed plants.

"What are you doing?" Danithia asked.

"I thought I'd help you out a little ..."

She looked at him, and a lump formed in her throat. She tried to clear it away. Tears welled in her eyes, and she fought hard not to let them fall. "Alex ..." she stopped. "Alex...I don't know what to do."

"Come home with me."

~ ~ ~

During the drive to his house, Danithia seemed distant, cold, and silent. Alex watched her as she stared out the window, her forehead touching the glass. She almost sat with her back to him, and that worried him. He hoped her body language wasn't a clear sign that she was inwardly turning away from him. He couldn't let that happen. He turned his attention to the road, where snow was beginning to accumulate into soft white piles here and there. He mentally surveyed his home, particularly his office, and hoped he had not left anything telling out that Danithia might see. He was usually very careful about such things, but frankly he hadn't anticipated having her as a house guest.

"Alex?"

"Hmm?"

"Where do you live?"

"I have a modest house in Montbello. Why do you ask?"

"Just wondering where you were taking me. Although, I guess, at this point it doesn't really matter, does it?"

"Of course it matters. Look, Danithia, would you rather go someplace else? I'll take you wherever you want to go."

She stared at him long and hard and tried to fight the demons of mistrust that held her captive. Did she really trust him? And if so, why? She didn't really know him, did she? For all she knew, he could be a rapist or a murderer. But once he returned her gaze, all those thoughts disappeared. And his tone of voice almost made her feel ashamed.

"No, Alex, there's no place else I want to go."

He released a huge breath of air, not realizing that he had been holding his breath. He wasn't even sure if he had wanted her to say yes or no. While she had sized him up, his mind was running through the rooms in his house, not only for tidiness, but also for carelessness.

He reached for and held her hand. "Once we get there, you can settle into a guest bedroom and I'll order a pizza. I even think I have some wine."

"That sounds fine. I forgot all about eating, but now that you've mentioned pizza, I'm ravenous."

And she really was. All of a sudden a knot deep inside herself started to untwist, and she felt better by simply letting go.

"I wonder how Pat is doing tonight?" she said wistfully, changing the subject.

"I suspect he's resting and being well taken care of."

"I can't believe he had a stroke. Now who's going to watch my back at the firm?"

"Why do you need somebody to watch your back?"

"Some of the partners want me off this case, and although I was able to fend them off last time, I don't know if I'll be able to do it again if they challenge me. After all, I'm just an associate."

"You're more than just an associate."

"Maybe to you, but certainly not to them. I just can't let Ms. Griffin down. I can't let that happen."

"Who's trying to stop you?"

"Lyle."

"McGregor?"

"Yeah, how did you know?" she asked, her voice rising with suspicion.

"I'm security, remember? I know all the names in the building."

"Welcome to my humble abode," he said cheerfully. "Let me just turn off the alarm and turn on some lights."

Once he had illuminated the house, Danithia saw a sparsely furnished living room decorated in shades of gray, a small wood table which held remnants of the morning's breakfast. No small appliances were on the counter tops in his large kitchen, not even a dish drain. His home was as non-distinct as was his office. No pictures on the walls, only a battery-powered clock. She watched him as he scurried about the room, picking up discarded pieces of clothing, a pair of shoes and dirty white socks. This is pitiful, she thought. Although, upon closer inspection, the house was beautiful. It had cathedral ceilings and glistening chandeliers in both the foyer and over the modest wood table in the dining area. The carpet was a dark forest green, the walls a lighter shade of green with white borders. With the right touches, she thought, this house could be a magnificent showpiece.

"Not into interior design, I see," she said and chuckled.

He laughed. "Obviously."

He took her bag and headed down a hallway toward the back of the house. She noticed that he closed doors along the way, surmising that he wanted her to stay away from those rooms.

"It gets pretty cold in here, so I keep the doors closed on unoccupied rooms. Let's the heat circulate better in the rooms that are occupied."

"Oh," she said.

"This will be your room tonight, madam." He bowed and moved his hand in a sweeping gesture as he let her pass him.

This room held a little more warmth, at least it had a little more personality. Although it had a modest bedroom set, the comforter was colorful, and stacks of fluffy pillows overpowered the bed. The night stand had a digital radio alarm clock and nothing more, except a small dish of butterscotch candy.

"You'll be comfortable in here," he said. "There's even a private bath. I'll go get you fresh towels."

Once he left the room, Danithia sat on the bed and removed her shoes. She rubbed the soles of her feet and ached for the embrace of slumber. She laid back on the inviting mound of pillows and closed her eyes. In fact, she started to doze, but her stomach growled and grumbled and she knew that she had to eat something or she'd never go to sleep peacefully. She ran over the events of the day in her mind and almost couldn't believe how much had happened in less than twenty-four hours. It felt as if an eternity had passed. She had accomplished a lot today, she saved Patrick, made an honest friendship with Patricia, but then everything turned ugly. Her house—her beautiful house—trashed, soiled, tarnished by someone's malicious hands. And Tanya was gone. Will I ever again feel safe in my own home? she wondered, as she closed her eyes and fought a fresh bout of panic.

~ ~ ~

Alex rushed past the linen closet and entered his office. He looked around the room at all the lavish equipment, state-of-the-art computer, a laser printer, fax machine, scanner, digitizer for processing CDs, two telephones sat on his desk. He swooped up some files and hurriedly stuffed them inside a file cabinet and locked the drawer.

In his haste he didn't notice the photograph that silently fell to the floor and wedged itself at the base of the cabinet.

He started to return to the guest bedroom. Snapped his fingers and turned back. He realized that he hadn't retrieved any towels. He was grateful that he'd recently bought new ones. Danithia will like these, he thought.

"Here you go!" he exclaimed, as he reentered the guest bedroom.

Startled, Danithia jumped, his booming voice rudely pushing her from her introspection.

"I'm sorry, I didn't mean to scare you."

"That's okay."

He looked at her face and saw lines of worry there. "Danithia, everything's going to be all right. Really, it will. Trust me."

"Do you think it'd be okay for me to take a shower while you order that pizza? I'm gritty and starving."

"Hmm, what an interesting combination. Should I have that put on the pizza?" he said, trying to make her laugh.

"Put anything on it you want, just get it here fast!"

"Yes, ma'am." He saluted, then left her alone.

She took her time, undressed slowly, almost timidly, glancing periodically at the door, as if she expected him to walk in even though she'd locked the door. But once she stepped inside the shower, she lost herself in the warm embrace of aquatic bliss.

~ ~ ~

Danithia finally emerged from the bedroom dressed in flannel pajamas and socks. She searched for Alex. There seemed to be more doors than she remembered. The hallway was dimly lit. She almost called out to Alex, then she heard a clicking, whirling noise coming from the room on her right. She stopped. She placed her ear against the door and heard the noises again. She looked around, then turned the knob.

A fax machine was spewing forth sheet after sheet of paper, and at first that didn't seem unusual until she really looked around the room. It was the most elaborate office space she'd ever seen. Two telephones! And what kind of machine was this, she wondered, as she stared at a rectangular shaped machine that was about the size of a laser printer, but wasn't. Why would Alex, a security officer, have equipment like this, she wondered? The file cabinet wasn't a run of the mill aluminum cabinet she was used to seeing. It was heavy metal, perhaps fire proof, its drawers extra large and each one had an elaborate seal around it. It was high tech, very security conscious. She ran her fingertips over the cold metal, fingering the seal. She looked down, then she saw a piece of paper sticking out under the cabinet. She bent to retrieve it. She looked at it and at first did not believe her eyes.

"What are you doing in here?" Alex said sharply.

She looked up at him, and her eyes shot daggers. "You know Lyle McGregor because you're security! Right!"

He saw the picture in her hand, and for a moment his heart stopped. Damn! Where'd that come from?

"Danithia, I can explain."

"Yeah, and well you better!"

"Let's go sit down, have some pizza and a glass of wine, and I'll explain everything to you."

"No!" she screamed. "I'm not going to go sit down and eat pizza and drink wine like nothing's going on here! Now tell me, how do you know Lyle?"

He struggled with himself for a moment and knew this had to be the moment of truth, and it was coming way too soon.

"Danithia, please understand."

"Understand what?"

He took a deep breath. "I'm not who you think I am."

"Who are you?" she said with growing alarm, realizing that she was inside his house, on a somewhat deserted street, far from her own element. Oh god, what if he's going to kill me?

"My name is Lewis—Lewis Alexander Powers."

"What! You even lied about your name!" Her eyes darted around the room looking for a weapon.

"Danithia, you've got to trust me. Let's go into the living room and sit down. I have a lot to tell you."

"Trust you!" she screamed. "Trust you! I must have been out of my mind to come here with you tonight. You're behind everything that's happened, aren't you?"

"No! No, you've got it all wrong."

"Ever since I laid eyes on you, my life has been going crazy."

"No," he corrected her, "it hasn't been that long."

"What's that supposed to mean?"

"The first time you laid eyes on me, you were wearing a white cashmere suit and you were drinking red wine."

She stood very still for a moment, her mind reeling. "You were at the fund-raiser for Senator Brown?"

"Yes."

"I don't remember seeing you."

"Many people don't notice who's waiting on them."

"You were a waiter?" she said, her brow wrinkling trying to remember.

"Yes."

"Let me get this straight. You were at Senator Brown's
fund-raiser and what . . . have you been stalking me since
then?"

He laughed aloud, and she feared she might be looking
at a lunatic.

"At first you weren't even my priority. In fact, you
weren't even thought of. And you can thank Ms. Griffin for
pulling you in."

"Hold up," she said, shaking her head. "What does
Patricia have to do with this?"

"See, I told you this would take a while, and we need
to sit down and discuss it."

She didn't budge but continued to stare at him as if he
were a monster.

"Danithia," Alex said. "Look at the photo again. Do
you recognize the other man?"

She stared at it, her eyes moving from the laughing face
of Lyle McGregor to another distinguished-looking gentleman with white hair. Lyle had his arm around him as the
two of them shared what resembled a conspiratorial laugh.

She looked up at Alex and whispered, "No, who is he?"

"Dr. Zimmerman."

Chapter 7

Danithia sat on the floor with her stockinged feet tucked beneath her. She consumed her second slice of pizza and sipped the glass of white zinfandel. Slowly the nourishment of her body helped her to no longer feel as if her world was spinning out of control. She could now attempt to absorb the enormity of the situation.

"Okay," she said. "I've had my pizza, and the wine has calmed me somewhat. Now, please stop the mystery and tell me what's going on?"

Alex gazed at her and wished there was a way to get back the trust he knew he'd lost, but he hoped with all his heart that after he shared with her the facts as he knew them, that she'd once again care for him the way she had before.

"In early 1996, one of the most influential men—a political powerhouse in Atlanta—disappeared without a trace. He was beginning to have a strong political voice, and his message of empowerment was going over very well in the Black community. He was becoming an icon, not unlike the powerful Dr. Martin Luther King, Jr. My organization was called in to investigate his sudden disappearance."

"Your organization? What organization is that?"

"Danithia, before I answer any of your questions you must realize that the information I give you is to be kept in the strictest confidence. Who I am and what I do is not to become common knowledge. You must promise me that you will not reveal any of this to anybody, or I simply can't go any further."

He stopped and studied her face. It was a mask of confusion, and he thought he saw disdain.

"You've got some nerve acting as if you can't trust me, when all along I shouldn't have been trusting you."

"Danithia, please, you must give me your word that everything I tell you tonight stays with you."

"Oh, all right. Just get on with the story."

"Say, 'I promise that the information revealed to me tonight will never be repeated.' Say it!" he demanded, his tone harsher than he'd meant it to be.

"I promise not to tell anybody anything about tonight. Okay?"

"Okay.

"I'm a federal agent. I work under the umbrella of the Federal Bureau of Investigation."

"The F-B-I!" she said dragging the initials, clearly astonished.

"There are many sub-agencies that work under the FBI and I am assigned to a special task force called 'Crimes of Vicious Ethnic Retaliation Taskforce,' code name COVERT."

"Covert! I've never heard of it."

"There are many things about the FBI and even the CIA that the average American knows nothing about. Frankly, you're not supposed to. Now, can I continue?"

"Yes, please, go ahead." Thoroughly intrigued, she settled more comfortably against the pillow at her back.

"Shortly after the disappearance of the gentleman in Atlanta, another Black man vanished. He was wealthy, one of the wealthiest men in the country."

"And your job is to find out what happened to them."

"Right. And I have. Through surveillance and various other covert means, we found out that both these men are not deceased, as first feared. Of course we suspected foul play, but neither family seemed to be grieving, there was no funeral, no request for assistance from the FBI for a possible kidnapping, nothing."

"Where are they?"

"They are alive and living in seclusion in their respective homes."

"So?"

"In the middle of 1996, another strong aspiring political figure here in Denver stopped campaigning and dropped out of the race when his chances of winning were very good."

"Are you talking about Senator Brown?"

"How did you know?"

"I'll tell you later. Keep talking."

"All these men—and now it also includes women—of color, either had strong economic power or political influence. And they all had one other thing in common."

"What was that?"

"Dr. Zimmerman."

Danithia sucked in her breath as everything came clearly into focus. "They all went into hiding because they're disfigured."

"Exactly."

"And Lyle, what's his role in all this?" she asked.

"I'm still not quite sure. You see, he didn't come into the picture until later, when the movement swung from unsuccessful attempts in California to Colorado, specifically Denver."

"What was the name of your task force again?"

"COVERT."

"No, tell me what that stands for again."

"Crimes of Vicious Ethnic Retaliation Taskforce."

"So you investigate crimes against certain ethnicities?" she asked.

"Crimes that are vicious in nature and seem to be aimed at a particular race, yes. And I bet you'd be surprised at just how many things happen directly as a result of racist motivations. COVERT was formed to identify those groups of people and dismantle them."

"So what happened to Ms. Griffin was a deliberate act?"

"Yes. She was targeted that evening, as were several others. I must tell you that you have a very courageous client in her. Everyone else who got tricked into using this cream chose to run and hide, making it very difficult for us to prosecute. She's the only one who had the good sense to find an ally, and she had the courage to fight."

"Do you know who the other people were that Dr. Zimmerman may have influenced that night?"

"Yes, in fact I know of a few."

"I believe Senator Brown was one of them. Can I get the names of the others from you?"

"Why?"

"They are potential plaintiffs for the class action. I've got to talk to them."

"I'll find out if I can tell you that. Okay?"

"You do that. There's no reason why I can't fight for them as well as Ms. Griffin."

"That's what I mean when I said you were an ally whom we weren't expecting. Unfortunately, Ms. Griffin's courageousness put you in the middle of our way."

"Oh, so I was bothersome to you all, huh?"

"You were only bothersome to me because you're so beautiful, and I've developed a fondness for you that makes my job just a tad bit more difficult."

"Why?" she said, smiling.

"Because you're distracting me, girl!"

She laughed, then turned serious.

"That night at the party, you knew Dr. Zimmerman would be there, right?"

"Right."

"How did you know that when Patrick didn't even know the man was there. He didn't invite him."

"We've been watching him for a while, and we've learned from other victims that he crashes parties where influential Black folks will be present."

"How does he get in?" she wondered.

"His credentials. And he's got plenty of 'em. He flashes his I.D. card, tells a story about misplacing his invitation, and people take one look at him, see a distinguished-looking gentleman—a doctor! And they let a monster waltz right into their midst."

"So you knew he was in Denver, you also knew about the party, so the taskforce put you there to what? Catch him?"

"To observe him, take snapshots, eavesdrop, etcetera."

"So you took the photo of Lyle and Dr. Zimmerman at the party?"

"No, that was taken in Simi Valley, California."

"What?"

"Sorry to break the news to you, but your boss is part of an organization that wishes to rid the world of uppity niggers, as I've heard him say."

"You've heard him say that!"

"Yep, with the assistance of some very fancy equipment and highly sensitized microphones positioned just right, you can easily record all conversations."

"So Lyle hates Black people, umm, umm, umm." Danithia absently took a sip of wine. "Now that you say it, it doesn't surprise me a bit."

"This organization is deadly, particularly as they grow more desperate to stop what they see as an invasion—a loss of their power.

"You know, the funny thing about all this is that when you think of the population of this country, only ten percent of it is Black and, to break it down even further, only about one percent of that ten is wealthy or powerful politically or otherwise. Now, why would that small number of people frighten them? I mean how much damage could they do?"

"Actually, when you think about it," said Danithia. "It doesn't take a massive amount of people to make changes, sometimes it takes only one. Look at Martin Luther King Jr., one man; Malcolm X, one man; John F. Kennedy, one man; and on the negative side, Adolf Hitler, one man."

He contemplated her statement and easily saw the wisdom in her reasoning. They both fell silent.

"I can see trying to humiliate and stop those people who were strong political forces, but why Ms. Griffin?" Danithia questioned. "She's only a writer."

"A writer, who has a large cross-over audience. A writer with economic power. Her stories are adored and consumed like hotcakes on Sunday morning. Think about it. With the small percentage of Blacks in this country, even if all of them bought her novels, there is still not enough of us to make her as wealthy as she is. I suspect Lyle's people didn't like her because they saw no value in what she does, yet others did and if they could stop her, make her disappear—vanish—like all the others from sheer humiliation, then that's one less person to worry about creeping up on them later. They're a paranoid bunch of folks."

"They're a vicious bunch of folks. Ms. Griffin didn't deserve this."

"Nobody did, but, Danithia, look at our society. It's so strongly influenced by White beauty. Let me ask you a personal question." He paused. "Did you ever want to be White?"

"Never!"

"Come on now, be honest."

"I am being honest. I'm proud of who I am!" she retorted indignantly.

"Okay, let's back up to your childhood. When you were a kid, what kind of dolls did you play with?"

"Mostly White, but I had a few Black dolls, too."

"Did you enjoy combing their long blond flowing hair?" he said, gesturing.

"Sure."

"What about your Black dolls, what kind of hair did they have?"

She thought for a moment and remembered how frustrated she used to get trying to style hair that was usually made of yarn.

"I get your point."

"When you watched television, what were the main images you saw in beauty contests, starring roles where men loved and adored the women, what kind of woman was it?"

"White."

"Exactly, and you mean to tell me that when you were a child you never wanted to be White?"

"I guess when you put it that way, I probably did. But it seems as though society made me want it, doesn't it?"

"Yes. And believe it or not, there are some people right now who would like nothing more than to have you still wanting it. People like Dr. Zimmerman and Lyle McGregor and their host of friends. Still craving that image, was the reason people like the gentleman in

Atlanta, Senator Brown, and even Ms. Griffin so easily fell
for the deception."

"I wish I could tell Patricia this so she could stop hating
herself. If she knew what an elaborate scheme this was,
she'd forgive herself."

"You can't tell her. I'm sorry. No matter what,
Danithia, you cannot tell her."

"But . . ."

"No buts, you promised. If COVERT were discovered,
I could no longer continue to do what I'm doing, nor could
any of the others. We're here to stop this malicious group,
and the operation is covert, and it must stay that way."

She shook her head, wishing there was something she
could do. But representing Ms. Griffin and the others was
the only contribution she could make.

"Am I in danger from Lyle?"

"I'm not sure. The incident in the elevator and the
lights-out thing, I suspect were of his doing. Probably nothing more than an attempt to frighten you. The vandalism
to your car and home takes it to another level. And frankly,
I'm not sure what it means. All I know for sure is that the
game is getting ugly and dangerous."

"This is a game to you?" she said.

"No baby, it's not a game to me, it's what we call an
assignment. 'Game' is a COVERT term."

"Did you ever find the surveillance tape that disappeared that night?"

"No, and that leads me to believe that a key person
appeared on it, and whoever played the lights-out game
with us, knew it and made sure we didn't see it."

"Looks like we missed a golden opportunity for discovery."

"Maybe not. Does Lyle have any children?"

"Yes, I believe he has two children, a daughter and a son."

"How old do you think the son is?"

"Oh maybe twenty, twenty-one."

"That could have been the blond-haired guy we saw on the tape."

"What makes you think that?"

"Remember, the blond-haired guy disappeared into the stairwell."

"Yes."

"You can't get out that way. You can only go up, and you can't enter one of the floors unless you have a key."

"Or," she said, "someone opens it for you."

"Right!"

"Bingo."

"I like the way you think." He grinned.

She looked at him for a long time. "I like what you do. It's very courageous, this COVERT operation. It seems that each minute I spend with you I begin to admire you more and more."

"Aw, shucks!" he said, bobbing his head up and down.

"But at the same time, I've had my moments of mistrust, too. And I want to apologize to you for that."

"Apology accepted. I understand that there was no way for you to know who to trust and who not to, with everything happening so fast."

"I knew you were more than a security guard."

"You did not."

"Okay, I didn't know it, but I sensed it." She paused. "Were you watching me at my house, the night I walked Tanya?"

"Yes."

"Why?"

"I shouldn't have been there. I was just watching, trying to gauge if you were in danger, especially after the scratch on your car—your first warning. I wanted to make sure no one harmed you."

"Why did you care about me?"

"I remember the first night I met you."

"At the party?"

"Well, it sort of started at the party, even though I didn't talk to you that night. Mainly I watched Dr. Zimmerman work the room. But I noticed you, and I thought you were beautiful, had a really nice sense of style about you, and I loved your Afro."

"Thank you."

"I think that was the first time since I've been a part of COVERT that I wished I could be someone else, doing something else, just so I could talk to you and have you accept me."

"I would have accepted you. I'm not a snob."

"That night I was pretending to be a waiter. Come on now, you would not have accepted any advances I sent your way. Don't even tell that lie."

She laughed. "Maybe not, I don't know. I do think that if I had noticed you I would have liked what I saw, and I might have flirted with you, but to be honest, my career up until this point hasn't allowed for much romance. I would have been a bitter disappointment to you in that respect."

"No time for romance, that's a damn shame," he said, shaking his head.

"Not really. I set some goals for myself, and I've accomplished a good many of them." She cocked her head to one side, giving him a flirtatious smile. "I could pursue something romantic now, I think."

"Oh, so you'll give a brother some play now that you know he ain't broke, huh?"

"From the looks of the furnishings in this house, you sho act broke, if you ain't," she said, imitating his use of bad grammar.

"Oh, so now you going to dog my place."

"Hey, I'm just telling you like it t-I-izzz."

"I've got an idea, you can decorate my house."

She laughed aloud. "Do I look like an interior designer to you?"

"No, but you do look like the kind of precious ornament I'd like to admire every single day. You would be my beautiful Black queen, and I'd build a throne just for you to sit upon, and I'd wait on you hand and foot, anything to please my lady love."

He quickly closed the distance between them and took her in his arms.

"I don't know what you're doing to me," he said, holding her. "But I'm as serious as a heart attack, and that scares the hell out of me."

"You'd really worship me every day, even with funky breath and messed-up hair and days of a vicious attitude?"

"I would give you a toothbrush and a comb, then I'd go pick a rose, hand it to you, and your attitude would disappear."

"You've got an answer for everything, don't you?" She stroked his cheek.

"Not everything, but I'm willing to work and learn and grow, and I believe I can do that with you."

"Come here," she whispered.

He kissed her passionately, then took her hand and led her from the living room. "I've got a surprise for you. Close your eyes."

"What kind of surprise?"

"This!" he said and threw open the door to his bedroom.

"Oh my goodness, isn't this nice," she exclaimed.

The master bedroom was more like a suite. In its center stood a round bed with a netted canopy partially encircling it. The bedding was an animal print, and there were at least a dozen pillows on it in various shades, sizes, and textures. There was a big-screen television nestled in one corner, with four overstuffed animal-print chairs facing it, a bearskin rug in the center. And across from that was a fireplace where a large black ceramic cougar, a paw reaching out as if to swipe you, graced its mantle. An open bar glistening with different bottles of expensive liqueurs, bourbon, and cognac, was on the other side of the room. And nestled in the farthest corner was a spiral staircase.

"Where does that lead?" she asked, pointing at the stairs.

"Come on, I'll show you." He took her hand but gestured for her to climb the stairs first.

They led up to a small deck with an uncurtained picture window that allowed you to view the city and the mountains beyond. There was a telescope, too.

"Very nice," she said, awed.

"Thank you."

"Can I look through the telescope?"

"Of course. If you don't move it, it should be positioned so you can gaze at the closest planet to the earth."

"Oh," she crooned. "That's beautiful. What planet is it?"

"You're looking at Mars," he said. "I love studying the planets. It's my favorite thing to do late at night."

"Really," she said, impressed.

"In fact, what I just said isn't exactly accurate."

"What are you talking about?"

"Venus and Mercury are planets within the Earth's orbit. So, they are the closest planets to Earth."

"Ahh. Where's the moon tonight?"

Gently, he pulled her from the telescope and gazed into her eyes.

"It's downstairs."

He took her in his arms and just held her. He enjoyed the feel of her in his arms, her softness against his bulk. The smell of her freshly scrubbed skin and whatever it was she put in her hair, all sent his mind reeling to heaven.

She stood on tiptoe and whispered in his ear, "Which planet is the farthest away from earth, do you know?"

"Pluto. Why?"

"That's where I want to go, Alex. Take me there."

He cradled her face in his hands, closed his eyes, eager to taste her lips and feed her soul. He placed closed-mouth kisses upon her lips, brushing back and forth, enjoying the contours of his full lips against her smaller mouth. Her mouth opened slightly, urging him to go deeper. He tickled her lips with his tongue, first the upper, then the lower. He circled around inside the inviting warmth of her mouth, swept his tongue lightly across her teeth, and continued to circle round and round her mouth, fanning her desire, their tongues touching and dancing a sensual form of tango.

He encircled her in his arms, his hands splayed open, supporting her should she lose her balance. His hands moved ever so slowly down the base of her spine to rest suggestively at that space where her sensual round bottom began—the one he had coveted with desire since seeing her walk her dog so long ago. He couldn't help but grip her bottom with power that was somehow delicate, urging her v-shaped mound to rest against the warmth of bulge between his legs.

Danithia sighed. She was spinning, spinning out of control, filling up with desire, wanting more of what he had to offer because she could tell he could take her to a level of ecstasy that until now she had never experienced. This kiss was not just a kiss, it was a prelude to an act she knew would declare him a master at the art of love. Having him so near her secret place caused a rush of liquefied emotion to dampen her panties. At this moment it seemed she wanted nothing more than to have him deep within herself, rocketing her to his moon, riding on a spaceship of love. As he fondled and caressed her thigh, she raised her leg and finally felt the bulk of him pulsating against her.

He gently settled her on the floor, atop a throw blanket he kept up there for chilly nights when he gazed at the stars. He took her in his arms again and, somehow, the clothes they wore seemed to disappear piece by piece with each kiss they placed upon each other.

Danithia was now naked and ready to begin the act of love. Alex paused, grabbed his pants, and for a split second Danithia feared he had come to his senses and changed his mind. But she watched as he fished in his pockets, retrieved his wallet, and produced a small tin-foil packet she knew to be a condom.

"I hate wearing these things, but I want to keep you safe."

"How about if I show you a way to at least enjoy putting it on."

He raised his eyebrows suggestively and handed the packet to her.

"Lie down," she demanded.

She straddled her naked body over his and made a great showy display of opening the wrapper, her breasts jiggling slightly with the motion of ripping it open. She held it in the air as if inspecting it for holes, then she held it against her closed mouth and then she smiled.

"What are you going to do?" he asked, watching her with fascination. He feared he would explode before he could enter her, because watching this performance was seductive as hell!

"This!" she said and bent over his manhood. She had placed the condom in her mouth, somehow holding it in position with the tip of her tongue. With a swiftness that surprised him, she had his member inside her mouth, the condom resting on its tip. She used her tongue and mouth to unravel it, rolling it down a portion of his shaft.

He closed his eyes and reeled with pleasure. The warmth of her mouth against the coolness of the latex was more sensual than anything he had ever experienced. He almost cried out an expletive that would adequately describe his joy.

Using her hands, Danithia finished the job, running her fingers down the full length of him—and what length he had. If it wasn't for the fact that she wanted him so badly she might have feared what his greatness could do to her. However, trepidation was quickly replaced with an intense desire to see how much of him she could take. She raised herself up by the palms of her hands, running her tongue up his belly and chest to suckle his nipple. She heard him groan aloud. Hearing his cries of ecstasy sent her desire and self-control packing. She was already straddling him and could feel the tip of him jumping and jerking, lightly grazing her. She reached for him with one hand, kissed him with hot, urgent kisses, then eased him into her, little by little, inch by glorious inch, until at last, she knew she had received all of him.

She could barely talk or even think, the feeling of him was so great and powerful and wonderful, but she managed to utter in a hoarse whisper, "Alex, take me to heaven."

And he did. In his arms, making sweet, sweet love, she felt as if he was on a mission to fly her to places where very few women had ever gone before. They became one, rocking each other with a strong, driving force like that of a space shuttle. With each endearing stroke, she imagined they were on a serious mission, making their first stop Mars, then they sailed away, ricocheted to Saturn, where she actually saw rings of bright, beautiful light encircling her. Then Jupiter whizzed by, and this great planet actually seemed tiny. They cruised by Pluto, making their last stop Earth, where warmth and sensual pleasure resides, where lovers make babies, and utterances of love echo with soft sighs and eager cries, and promises are easily made. She came back to Earth and found herself smack dab in the middle of Alex's paradise.

Chapter 8

As the sun began to rise, Danithia snuggled deeper under the covers, wriggling her butt, backing up until she was touching Alex. He turned and embraced her, throwing his leg over her, pulling her into him.

"Good morning," he whispered into her ear.

"That tickles."

"What tickles?"

"Your breath directly in my ear."

"Want some breakfast?"

"This early?"

"No, later, after we wake up again."

"Smart man, you knew I was going back to sleep."

"Nope, I knew I wanted to rock you back to sleep."

"Alex," she said, dragging his name. "I can't spend all day making love."

"Why not?"

"Because I've got a job to go to."

"Danithia, after all that happened to you yesterday, don't you think you deserve to take the day off? Besides, we need to bury Tanya."

She didn't want to think about Tanya. The loss of her beautiful dog brought buried pain to the surface. Frankly, there were many things about yesterday she did not want to remember, except, of course, her wonderful night of discovery with Alex.

"What do you say?" he asked.

"I think you're right. I need a day to recover. I'll call Valerie and let her know I won't be in." She snuggled closer to him. "I'd normally let Patrick know when I wasn't

going to make it. Since he's in the hospital, I should probably call Lyle, but I sure don't want to, not now that I know
about him," she said, her tone angry.

"You've got to act as if you don't know, Danithia. Call
him. Don't raise any suspicions by doing something out of
the ordinary, like not following protocol."

She turned over to face Alex.

"How can I look that man in the face knowing all that
he's cost me, Ms. Griffin, and countless other people? Tell
me how I do that and not spit in his eye?"

"Babe, I know it's going to be hard, but you've got to
find a way to tuck this information deep in the back of your
mind. Save it for later. Maybe we'll get to use it in Court.
Shock him, like one of those old Perry Mason flicks."

"Yeah, stick it to him in Court, point at him and say 'is
this the man?' And have him squirm in his seat, jump up,
and confess," she said, dramatizing the scene in her mind.

"Down girl, down girl." Alex patted her gently. "We're
going to get him."

Suddenly her expression turned from vindictive to one
of sadness.

"What's wrong?" Alex asked.

"I used to always have to tell Tanya to get down, now
I'll never get to do it again." She covered her face with the
blanket as tears began to form in her eyes.

"She was a good dog. How do you feel about getting
another one?" Alex asked.

"It would be like betraying her, Alex, I can't replace her
that easily."

"I'm sorry, baby. I didn't mean to be insensitive by sug-
gesting that. God, what was I thinking!" he said, slapping
his forehead with the palm of his hand.

She took his hand, turned it over, and placed a soft kiss in his palm. Then she ran her lips over his knuckles, kissing them, before placing his palm against her cheek.

"You feel so good," said Alex. "So soft." The dampness that moistened her cheeks felt special, for he was touching her tears. Silently, he vowed he'd find a way to make her happy and make Lyle McGregor, Dr. Zimmerman, and everybody else involved pay.

Caressing him, she placed her cheek on his bare chest and listened to the melodious harmony of his beating heart.

"Your heart's beating really fast," she said.

"Yeah? Well, it's a wonder it's not bursting out of my chest, with you stroking me like that."

She lifted the covers and climbed atop him, straddled his thighs, and gazed into his eyes. She gyrated against him and rubbed his chest with firm strokes.

He could barely speak, but managed to say, "What a way to start the day!"

"Sho you right!" she said as the love game began all over again. This time there were no planets, she just saw about a million tiny, sparkling stars.

~ ~ ~

Once they arrived at Danithia's house, she had to resist the urge to flee. She was afraid to enter her own home, but with Alex's hand firmly wrapped around hers, she gathered strength from him. But in the backyard, as soon as she saw the lifeless mound of Tanya under the blanket, she had to stop to catch her breath.

"I'll do this if you can't handle it, babe," Alex said.

"No, I want to help. I've got to say goodbye."

"You're sure?"

"I'm sure. Let me get the shovel. I think I want to bury her over there, near this tree she liked so much." She paused and took several deep breaths. "Do you think the ground will give okay?"

"It's not frozen. It'll be a little solid, but I can do it."

They worked for nearly an hour. The hole was quite a bit larger than Danithia anticipated, but Alex told her it had to be to accommodate Tanya's body, stretched out and stiff as it was.

"Ready?" he asked.

"Okay." She stepped back, crossed her arms around herself like a shield, and braced herself.

He gathered the bundle in his arms, careful to keep the blanket securely tucked around the dog. He laid her down as gently as he would a sleeping baby, and the sight of his tenderness brought fresh tears to her eyes.

Danithia couldn't watch as he threw the dirt and snow into the hole. The tears that had already formed, started to fall. Unable to continue to watch him, she stepped inside her kitchen and began to clean, not allowing her mind to think or dwell too much on her loss. She moved mechanically as if this were an everyday occurrence for her, removing food and containers from the floor, wiping down her cabinets, putting canned goods back on the shelves. She saw Alex when he came in, but she didn't acknowledge him. He said nothing, just picked up a broom and began to sweep the floor. They worked together like that, going from room to room, speaking very little, until their tasks were done.

"Boy, I'm getting hungry," she heard herself say, and then she smiled at him.

"What would you like?" he asked.

"You," she said suggestively, "on a plate, so I can sop you up like syrup on a biscuit."

He smiled and was glad to see that her mood had lightened. He'd learned long ago that when a woman's hurting, you've got to let her go through that hurt, and when she's good and done, she'll be back and she'll thank you for not getting in her way.

"Now that can be arranged. Hand me one of them plates!" He started to unzip his pants and said, "You think I'm playing!"

She laughed and gathered him in her arms and whispered, "Thank you."

"For what? Being willing to be devoured like a biscuit?"

"No, for being you. I'm thankful you're here with me. It's helped ease a lot of my pain."

He kissed the tip of her nose. "You're welcome. Actually, there is no other place I'd rather be right now than here with you. Now," he said cradling her face in his hands, "let's go eat."

~ ~ ~

They headed toward lower downtown, the home of Larimer Square and nearby Coors Field. Locals called this area "LoDo" for lower downtown. Danithia could recall when this area was considered skid row, bums and derelicts littering the streets almost as plentifully as the discarded newspapers and soda pop cans. Now, it was a thriving business community with posh restaurants, vintage clothing stores, and numerous breweries.

They had lunch at The Chop House, an elegant restaurant which had excellent food. Their specialty was steaks, but the menu boasted a wide variety of foods, including seafood. Each cherrywood table had a white table cloth and fresh-cut exotic flowers. Danithia loved the unique quirkiness of the Chop House, particularly since its elegance was sharply contrasted by casually dressed diners. It was an interesting mix, and the only reason this worked was because of the location. This was the place people came to enjoy a delicious meal after a Rockies game, so you'd see semi-formal attire right next to someone wearing a t-shirt and shorts.

After they enjoyed their meal she suggested that they go over to Coors Field.

They walked hand in hand. It was rather cold after last night's snow flurries, evidence that winter's kiss was soon to be upon them. In fact, Thanksgiving was right around the corner. They crossed Blake Street and trotted over to Coors Field. This newly structured ball park was home to the Colorado Rockies, and it was built reminiscent of old-time baseball fields. It was painted in shades of purple and teal, the colors of the Rockies. Since this wasn't baseball season, the field wasn't open but they could see through the steel gates. The outside parameters had numerous shops for buying sports memorabilia, including clothing of the city's football team—the Broncos—as well as plenty of things sporting the Rockies logo.

They continued to walk around until they came across the Sandlot Brewery, which was open. They went inside to get warm. Immediately upon entering, there was a very distinct odor, not unpleasant, just different. Danithia wrinkled her nose and wondered what it was.

There were three huge silver vats behind a glass enclosure. They walked up the stairs and gazed at it. Steam rose from one of them. A man poured a mixture into a paper cup and sipped its contents.

"Ugh," Danithia said, "I bet that's nasty, hot beer!"

"He's probably testing the fermentation. Why don't you go down there and ask him what he's doing. See if he'll give you a sip."

"I don't want to taste it, but I'll find out what he's doing."

A few minutes later she returned, a triumphant look on her face.

"Hey," she said, "look what I've got for you."

"What's that?"

"A new beer they're testing and he wants to know what you think of it."

"I'll taste it, if you do, too."

Although Danithia despised the taste of beer, she tried it anyway. It was a red beer that was described as full bodied and flavorful. She pronounced it just plain old nasty.

Alex laughed at her, "I thought you only made faces like that when you're in bed in the throes of passion. Now I'm not so sure passion was what I was seeing last night."

"Shut up," she said. "How can you drink that awful stuff!" She wrinkled her nose as she watched him drink the rest of the beer in one gulp.

"It's the connoisseur in me," he teased. "Besides, how can you live in Denver and not be a fan of beer, particularly Coors beer. Why that's un-Denveritish."

"Pleeze," she said, "that's like saying living in Denver means you must be a Bronco fan, or be a skier. And that's just plain not true."

"Danithia, do you ski?"

"Yes."

"Do you love the Broncos?"

"Yes."

"I rest my case," he said chuckling.

Chapter 9

Danithia returned to the office. Everyone seemed to think she was some kind of hero, having heard about her life-saving actions at Patrick's house. Even Valerie was duly impressed. Danithia shrugged it all off as inconsequential. As far as she was concerned, she had a hunch, and had followed it. It was as simple as that. Later, she was thoroughly delighted when she received a call from Patrick.

"Danithia..." he slurred.

"Patrick!" she exclaimed.

"...thank you for helping me."

"You're welcome. I just wish I had come sooner. I had a feeling something was wrong, but several weird things happened here that threw me off track to finding out what was going on with you."

"How's the...Comex...case coming?"

"So far, okay. There have been some interesting developments." She paused not sure if she should fill him in with all the details.

"Such as?"

"Well, Lyle and several other partners asked me to stop litigating the case. They say it's too costly."

"That's absurd."

"I know. I was able to convince them to allow me to continue, and I didn't use a conventional way to do that."

"What's that mean?"

"Well, I kinda-sorta threatened them."

He chuckled. "That's my girl."

"I believe in this case. I want to help these plaintiffs, and I swear if I had to leave this firm to do it, I would have."

"No need to think that way. I'm behind you one hundred percent."

"Thank you, Pat. How are you feeling?"

"More a question of how I look. Seems my face wants to slide south," he said, his voice beginning to sound weary.

"Pat, there's so much I want to tell you, but I think you'd better get some rest. I'll come see you later. Is that okay?"

"Counting on it."

"I'll be there. Goodbye."

She held the receiver a moment longer and stared into space. She visualized his face, the way his left eye, cheek, and corner of his mouth had drooped and felt sorry that such a handsome man's face would be forever changed.

That made her think about the other possible plaintiffs in the Comex case. Alex had given her six names. Composing a brief introductory speech in her head, she dialed.

Five times she was rejected. She did not even get to speak to the people she hoped to represent, but was questioned suspiciously by whoever answered the phone, then was told that so-and-so could not come to the phone.

She hit pay dirt with her last and final call.

"Hello, my name is Danithia Gilberts. I am an attorney here in Denver, and I'd like to speak to Mr. Anderson, if he's available."

"This is Mr. Anderson, what can I do for you?"

Danithia was so surprised, she almost lost her composure. "Mr. Anderson, I'm calling to inquire about a matter of an extremely sensitive nature. I realize that you may not want to speak to me, but I hope that, if you'll give me five minutes of your time, I can help you."

"Help me?" He started to sound suspicious. "Help me with what, young lady?"

"Several months ago, one of the members of my law firm held a fund-raiser for Senator Brown. I understand you were a guest."

"Yes."

"At that event, one of my clients was approached by a Dr. Zimmerman."

She fell silent and waited for some type of response to the name. Hearing nothing, she continued. "My client fell victim to a vicious crime, orchestrated to induce her to change the color of her skin. And . . ." She paused. "I understand this same man was also speaking to you that evening."

She heard a long sigh, then a weak, "Yes."

"Yes?" she repeated.

"I spoke to him, too."

"Mr. Anderson, this is personal but very important. Are you . . . are you okay?"

"So far. I haven't begun to exhibit the physical trauma others have. I only had two treatments."

Danithia's heart hammered. "Mr. Anderson, would it be possible for us to meet?"

"I don't venture out of doors anymore. I fear the sun will hasten the process."

"May I come to you?"

"I don't know what I can do to help you. I'm trying desperately to reverse this process, and researching is taking up a great deal of my time."

"I understand. Have you consulted other physicians to counter the process?"

"Yes. But so far I've not had much luck, because first they must analyze the formula, find out what ingredients were used, and maybe then, once they have this information, they could prepare a counteracting formula. Unfortunately, I don't have any of the cream in my possession, and the clinic, as you probably already know, is no longer in business."

"Yes, I know it's closed. How are you doing the analysis?"

"I've allowed a lab to extract tissue samples from me."

"From your face?" she asked.

"No, they were able to scrape tissue from my neck and hands. They're analyzing that, but this process is time consuming. It would be so much easier if they had the cream."

"I see. Mr. Anderson, I am representing a class of people who are suing Dr. Zimmerman and a company called Comex Manufacturing. The purpose of my call is to inform you of this class action and to advise you that you can be a part of the class."

"At this point, I'm not interested in suing."

"You don't have to be concerned about the lawsuit, just be aware that in the event we are able to come to a settlement with Comex, you can benefit from a portion of the proceeds we collect."

"My main concern is reversing this process before I become hideously disfigured." He said, completely ignoring what she had just told him.

"Since you're not disfigured yourself, sir, how do you know that this will happen?"

"Let's just say I didn't go into this alone. I just started a little later than someone else I know."

"May I ask who that is?"

"You can ask, but I won't divulge that information. In fact, I'd like to know how you found me."

"I have the guest list for the party, and I've contacted lots of people, but I must say most are not willing to talk to me. So, I thank you for your time."

"Ms. Gilberts, this is something I'm not very proud of. I'd rather not have my name associated with this mess. I hope you can appreciate that fact and respect my wishes."

"As I said before. The purpose of my call is to make you aware of the lawsuit. It is within your right under the law, and anyone else you know of, to be a part of the lawsuit, having a silent participation. In fact, your name wouldn't even appear on any of the documents we file with the court."

"It wouldn't," he paused. "I'm not sure I understand what you're telling me."

"I'm simply advising you that you can benefit from any monies we collect by being a part of the class. But I certainly can respect the way you feel. May I just say one thing before I hang up?"

"Go ahead."

"At the risk of sounding like I'm standing on a soap box, I must tell you that this is an enormous wrong done to our people, and we can't sit back and hope that it will quietly go away."

"I'm not quietly watching this thing happen. I'm trying to do something about it."

"Yes, you are. But I'd venture to say that you are doing so on your own behalf, while there are quite possibly many, many more people in this same predicament. I don't know if you realize it or not, but there is a bigger picture to look at than just one individual."

"Such as?"

"There are millions of dollars at stake, lucrative careers, and fine reputations, such as the one I'm sure you have, that need restoring. Look, Mr. Anderson, all I'm trying to say is that it really only takes one brave soul to bring this to the light—to stand up and fight. I have one such person, and she would be considered the lead plaintiff. I'd like to have you as another. All I'm asking is that you think about it."

"I will, but my mind's pretty much made up on this subject."

"Will you let me send you a copy of the complaint we filed in U.S. District Court? Perhaps once you see the allegations and our demand for relief, you'll change your mind."

He acquiesced and gave her a post office box number to use. Satisfied, Danithia hung up and prepared a letter to Mr. Anderson. She was not going to take "no" for an answer.

~ ~ ~

"Valerie, can you please type this letter for me as soon as possible. I want to send it out today. Oh, and also include a copy of the Comex complaint with it."

"Sure, no problem. Hey, I wanted to congratulate you on saving Patrick's life. Being a hero has put a definite glow on you."

Danithia smiled at her, anxious to tell her about her evening with Alex. "Come into my office, I've got some stuff to tell you!"

Once the door was shut, Danithia turned around and blurted, "Girl, you will not believe the kind of day I had yesterday."

"I can imagine it was scary."

"Scary, yes. But finding Patrick was not all that happened. When Alex took me home, my house was in shambles, somebody had broken in."

Valerie's eyes grew wide. "For real!"

"But that's not the half of it." Danithia's throat tightened. "Whoever it was, killed Tanya."

"Oh no. Not Tanya wont-stop-jumping-up-on-people Tanya."

"She won't be jumping on anybody anymore."

"Oh, girl, I'm so sorry to hear that. What is going on? All of a sudden it seems your life is getting crazy."

"I know. But Alex made everything a whole lot better."

"Alex, security-guard Alex?"

"You know who he is. Stop playing."

"So you finally hooked up with him."

"Boy, did we hook up!"

"Oh, oh, what's that mean?" Valerie teased her.

"It means exactly what you think. Girl, that man can make love to you so intense, he'll make you forget your own mama's name!"

"Damn! I have to admit he did look like he had it going on."

"He is so wonderful, I mean everything about him is perfect. I found myself doing things with him and to him that I'd have to be dating a man a long time before I'd venture down those erotic roads. But not with him, no. Oooh, gurl...he make ya wanna sang!"

"That good, huh? Must be nice. While I'm trying to forget my last sexual disaster, you're bragging about him like he's some kind of love god or something."

Danithia smiled. A love god? Indeed.

~ ~ ~

Later that evening, Danithia waited in the corridor for Alex to get off work. Since the break-in, she'd been staying at his house. She felt comfortable there, and for the first time in her life she enjoyed going home with someone, cooking for him, sharing her life with someone. She told herself not to get too comfortable with the situation, but each day it got easier and easier. Alex opened up a whole new world of discovery for her. His vast knowledge of so many things always fascinated her. He'd tell her stories about his various on-the-job escapades, he'd enlighten her on the planets, astrology, astronomy, astrophysics, and he was an excellent cook. Little by little, she found herself filling his home with her things. First it was her plants. She couldn't let them stay in her house unattended, so she brought them to his. She had minored in horticulture and longed for the day she could have her own greenhouse. Alex suggested she start one in a back room that was full of sunlight and had lots of windows. Together, in the spring, they would buy seedlings for flowers, fruits, and vegetables. She even wanted to buy a small orchid. She felt so at home with her hands deep in rich, brown soil or plucking weeds from her plants. She couldn't wait to nourish and baby tomato plants and she was excited to see if she could grow her own mustard and collard greens. She envisioned having several neat little rows of plants growing everywhere and each one she would give full attention and much love.

They enjoyed Thanksgiving Dinner with her family, and everyone instantly liked him. She was so surprised that her brothers did not interrogate him, instead, they welcomed him with open arms. After dinner, all the men played a game of tag football, and she watched with fascination as a bond began to form between her brothers, her father, and Alex. That was a first. Later, when she and Alex were alone, and she told him how lucky he was not to have been bitten down by her brothers, all he said was that this was a good omen—a sign that maybe things should become permanent. She was speechless.

Chapter 10

The day for the deposition of Patricia Griffin had arrived. Danithia picked her up. As they drove, she again briefed Patricia on what to expect. She quickly went over everything again, in an effort to not only prepare her client, but also to calm her own jittery nerves.

Patricia was ready—nervous—but ready. She had practiced and rehearsed telling her story again and again so as not to appear seeking pity, only a semblance of understanding. Patricia knew their goal was to paint a clear picture of victimization, but she had never, ever thought of herself in those terms—and she didn't want to think that way now. Even though she knew this was a legal tactic, it didn't sit well with her. She had made a not-too-smart decision and, no matter what happened today, it would stay with her the rest of her days. No, she had come to terms with her mistake and now all she wanted was to have her say, face the people she was accusing of maliciously harming her, and then, maybe, she could get on with picking up the pieces of her life.

Danithia and Ms. Griffin entered the conference room of Danithia's law firm. Already present in the medium-sized conference room were the three lawyers representing Comex, a court reporter, and, Mr. Gallagher, the President and CEO of Comex. At first there had been minor chatter among the people in the room, good mornings and casual banter. But once Danithia appeared with the black-cloaked figure with her, all conversation ceased. The court reporter's mouth fell open, and all eyes were conspicuously on Patricia. Danithia knew she must feel very uncomfortable. She ushered her to the deponent's chair, directly in front of the video camera—the camera she tried to have removed as Patricia had requested, but the defendants' counsel had insisted that the proceedings be taped. She seated herself next to Patricia, and calmly interlaced her fingers.

"Gentlemen," Danithia began, rising to her feet, "my client is here today to answer any reasonable and pertinent questions you might have. I have advised her that, if there are any improper inquiries or questions that seem combative in nature, I shall instruct her not to answer, and we can discuss and resolve the question's relevance either here or later before a judge. With that said, we can begin with the deposition."

One of the lawyers rose. "Good morning, Ms. Griffin."

"Good morning."

"My name is Peter Ivy and I represent one of the defendants in this action, Comex Manufacturing. Today, I will ask you a series of questions regarding the claims outlined in your Complaint against my client and try to establish the basis for those claims and accusations. Did anyone help prepare you for the testimony you will give today?"

"Yes, my lawyer did. Danithia Gilberts."

"Anyone else?"

"No, sir."

"Okay. Let's begin. Would you please state for the record, your full name, and please spell it, your home address, including your telephone number, and place of business."

Patricia answered the questions in a monotone voice, while deep inside she was bracing herself for the hard questions she knew were coming.

Satisfied with her answers, he then asked a series of questions regarding her educational background, then switched to questions about her work, her success as a writer, and her current estimated annual income, to which Danithia strongly objected. Income was not relevant, nor would it lead to the admission of relevant evidence. Ms. Griffin, as instructed, did not answer.

Danithia watched everyone in the room, gauging each one of their reactions to Ms. Griffin, her demeanor, and her ability to articulate her responses in a well-defined, reasonable manner. She noticed that everyone, with the exception of the reporter and Mr. Ivy, seemed to feel the need to study their blank yellow legal pads rather than keeping their eyes on Ms. Griffin. This was good in Danithia's opinion. If lawyers had trouble facing Patricia, a jury certainly would too, and a jury would have a level of empathy and sympathy for her that could easily turn a verdict in their favor.

Danithia was so busy surveying the players in the room that she almost missed an improper question. She saw Ms. Griffin visibly squirm in her chair.

"Would you repeat that question, please?" Danithia asked, interrupting the proceedings.

"Ms. Griffin, are you ashamed of being Black?"

"Objection! Irrelevant!" Danithia said sharply.

"The question is relevant. It pertains directly to her state of mind."

"I reiterate, objection! Irrelevant."

"With all due respect, Ms. Gilberts, it is relevant. It is our contention that her state of mind—her inability to accept her Blackness—led her to take such drastic measures. Please instruct your client to answer."

Danithia glared at him. "Objection. Period. End of discussion."

"Ms. Gilberts, if we have to conduct this deposition before a court-appointed third party, then we will. I strongly believe the question to be relevant, and I want her to answer it!" Peter Ivy banged his open palm on the table.

Danithia rose. "You are not to try intimidating my client. I will not stand for it. She's been through enough. If you continue with this line of questioning, I intend to end this deposition right here, right now."

The two glared at each other. The court reporter, hands poised over the keys of her machine, nervously looked from one to the other.

"Danithia," Ms. Griffin said, "I can answer his question. In fact, I want to answer it. Please allow me to."

"Patricia, you don't have to. Let me handle this."

"No!" Patricia's voice rose. "I want to answer it. I want them to know what led to this tragedy."

Danithia stared at her and decided to let her client speak her mind.

Mr. Ivy watched this exchange with a smirk on his face. "Please answer the question, Ms. Griffin."

"Could you repeat it, please?" Ms. Griffin asked.

"In all honesty, I'm not sure how I worded the question. Could the court reporter please read back that question?"

There was silence for a moment. Danithia remembered the question, and she hated it.

"Ugh, the question was: 'Are you ashamed of being Black?'"

"No," Ms. Griffin replied.

"Excuse me," Mr. Ivy interjected. "Did you say 'no?'"

"You heard me correctly."

"Then pardon me," he said, straightening his tie. "if you're not ashamed of being Black, why did you try an experimental formula to make you White?"

"Objection. That question is combative, irrelevant, and most of all, reprehensible!" Danithia said.

"They don't get it, do they, Danithia? They think I was trying to be White!" Ms. Griffin said, astonished. "My dear misguided young man, this was not an attempt to become White, this was an attempt to simply bleach the tone of my skin to a lighter shade of brown. I have never wanted to be White. In fact, I ask you, why would I want that?" She looked genuinely perplexed. "The reputation of the White race is one I would never want to be connected with. Your race despises and scorns and punishes other people because they are different. Whites have caused some of the most heinous crimes and have been part of the most vile things to ever happen in the history of this country. And you think I wanted to be associated with that! I tried to change my appearance because I lacked the appreciation for who I am, who my ancestors were. But I should have ultimately been proud of all that I am. I let Dr. Zimmerman and Comex take from me the one thing I should have been proud of—and never tried to change—and that is my Blackness."

The room was quiet after her emotional outburst as everyone sat silently absorbing her words.

"Danithia," Patricia began again. "Bless you child for trying to help me, but I've got to do something you don't really want me to."

Danithia looked at her and wondered what she could possibly be talking about. Then, when she saw Ms. Griffin rise, she instinctively knew.

"This case is not about despising blackness in favor of whiteness. It is about a malicious act that has left me trapped, hiding beneath a shroud. Do any of you realize how awful that can be?" Patricia slowly looked around the room at all their faces. "Can you imagine not being able to write, or work, or simply breathe without knowing—each and every second—that you've allowed someone to do something awful to you? Can you?"

She stopped, her breathing harsh and quick. She bent, gathered the hem of the cloak in both hands, then pulled it over her head.

A gasp came from each person. The court reporter knocked over her tiny machine as she fled the room. Mr. Ivy sat down, visibly shaken, and would not look up again. His pale face turned even more pale, and he looked as if he might pass out.

Tears welling in her eyes, Ms. Griffin turned to the camera. She tried to speak through her sobs. "I...no longer...want to be light. I never wanted to be White. Now all I want to be is me again. That's all I want." Tears streamed down her marred face. "That's...all...I...want."

Danithia stood up, fighting tears herself. She took Patricia in her arms and attempted to soothe her. She patted her back, whispering, "Everything will be okay."

Sobbing, Patricia replied, "It'll never be okay. Never, ever again."

~ ~ ~

As Danithia comforted Ms. Griffin, both Lyle McGregor and Gerald Primes came out of their offices. As they approached the open conference room door, they saw Danithia talking to a horribly disfigured woman. With raised eyebrows, they exchanged looks, then swiftly left the area.

~ ~ ~

By the end of the business day, a written offer for fifteen million dollars came to Danithia via a faxed letter. She raised an eyebrow but thought, you're not even close to what we want. She knew that, if they went to trial and Ms. Griffin showed herself again, they'd be paying an awful lot more than fifteen million. That was pocket change as far as she was concerned. Not only did this offer not take into consideration pain and suffering, loss of earnings, and malicious damages, it didn't even consider the other victims. And Danithia's gut told her there would be many, many more. Danithia had hired a damage expert, and his estimation came to at least fifty million dollars each. Danithia thought, God help 'em if we find all the plaintiffs.

She made a note to have somebody find out how much it would cost to run ads in all the newspapers around the country especially all the small African American trade magazines and newspapers. Those notices should generate some response. Surely not everyone affected felt too humiliated to come forward.

She phoned Ms. Griffin. "Patricia, we've got an offer."

"That was fast."

"It may have come fast, but it falls way short of what it should be."

"I don't even care to know what it is, then. If you think it's not enough, simply tell them 'no thanks.' I trust your judgment. Besides, as you know, it's not about the money anyway."

"Will do. And Patricia, I just wanted to tell you how brave I thought you were today."

"I wasn't after bravado. This whole thing is so ludicrous, from me subjecting myself to such humiliation, to them thinking it's about me wanting to be White. I feel so stupid."

"Doesn't it make you feel a little better to know that you're not the only one. That there are others, maybe lots of others?"

Patricia sighed. "Not really. Only time and God will heal my many wounds."

"And a guilty verdict for the defendants would be good too, right?" Danithia encouraged.

"Right."

~ ~ ~

Danithia quickly dictated a letter of reply, acknowledging their offer with a polite "we cannot accept." She didn't give them a counteroffer either. That would get their attention because, she knew instinctively they did not want to go to trial. In fact, this strategy of noncommittal was quite enjoyable. She liked knowing they would be squirming.

~ ~ ~

At midnight, Lyle McGregor, Gerald Primes and Franklin Ditz, were in a closed door meeting, their discussion getting louder and more intense.

Lyle attempted to quiet them. "Gentlemen! We cannot allow this small setback to cause us to fight among ourselves."

"Small setback!" Gerald cried. "Aren't you taking this just a little too lightly?"

"Bad choice of words. I apologize. I simply meant that regardless of what happened today in that deposition, no matter what we've seen, we've got to hold our ground and remain calm. Collectively we made this decision to become involved, and we've got to stick to it."

"I agreed to harmless scare tactics, not hideous deformity!" Gerald hissed.

"Look, don't act as if you can't get your hands dirty now." Lyle gave him a look of disgust. "Regardless of how bad she or any of them look, we've got to stay focused on our goal."

"And what is our goal?" Franklin asked sarcastically. "To rid the United States of any and all economic and political threats from any non-White persons? Not only is that notion ridiculous, I think it's impossible! There are far too many of them now."

"Lyle," Gerald chimed in. "I agree with Frank, this thing is way out of control. I saw that woman today, and never in my life have I felt so ashamed for . . . for . . . knowing that I have something to do with her injuries."

"You had nothing to do with her injuries!" Lyle shouted. "She did it to herself. She willingly agreed to the treatment. It's not our fault it backfired."

"It is our fault and you know it. Don't play games with words Lyle. It's one thing to pretend with everybody else, it's quite another to do that with us."

"We did not make that formula," Lyle countered, incredulous that they felt the need to take on so much blame. "In fact, we had nothing whatsoever to do with it."

"We may not have manufactured it, but, as lawyers, we know we'll be considered accessories. We helped conceal the crime. Even though we weren't there when it happened, we're accomplices. It's as simple as that," Gerald said in a defeated tone of voice.

"Yep." Frank reached for his briefcase, "And the fact that we had no knowledge of how extensive the damages would be is irrelevant. We may as well have administered the cream ourselves, 'cause we're guilty as hell."

"I want out," Gerald said, jumping to his feet.

Lyle stared at him for so long that Gerald began to fidget.

Clutching his briefcase, Frank rose. "Me too."

Lyle's face turned purple. "You don't just walk away from this organization—from our mission!"

"Watch me!" Frank shouted. "You may be adamant about this, and although I was too at one point in time, I'm not anymore and I'm getting out. Right here, right now!"

The room was quiet, each man consumed with his own thoughts.

Lyle watched them for a time, drumming his fingers absently across the table. "Okay. I'll agree that we're all guilty, that we'll be convicted if we're ever tried for this mess, but that's a big IF! We're silent partners in this. No one really knows about our participation but us. We can't walk away, but maybe we can step aside, at least until things cool down."

Lyle looked around and was met with solemn expressions and haunted eyes. "Look, I don't know how we got so unlucky that the Griffin woman would go to one of our own attorneys for representation, but this case should never have been accepted. Damn that Danithia with her self-righteous ways and bold determination! I'd like to smear some of that cream on her face! See what happens when you let one of them in your midst!"

"Lyle, you can spout all the racist B.S. you want. The bottom line is Patrick hired Danithia because she's a good lawyer and, up until now, she's always served the interests of this firm the way we wanted her to. Don't get nasty now 'cause your balls are in a sling."

"Correction," Lyle interrupted. "Our balls is more accurate."

Gerald squirmed in his seat and wrung his hands. "And all those things you did to her to make her leave this case alone backfired. But what I want to know is why your son killed her dog. That was uncalled for," Gerald said with disgust.

"He's a sick little bastard, you know that, Lyle," Frank said.

"How dare you speak of my son like that. The dog bit him, for god's sake. He didn't mean to kill the dog, just defend himself against it. Besides, I'm the one who's at the most risk. Try keeping a dog bite and the possible admission of rabies shots a secret. And my wife! Dammit, don't

even make me think about her nagging questions and suspicious nature. Women!"

Frank stalked toward the door. "I never, ever, would
have gotten into this had I known it would go this wrong.
Never!"

"Me either," said Gerald, following in Frank's wake.

~ ~ ~

Meanwhile, the tiniest of microphones, attached to a leaf
in a potted plant, had picked up every word the three men
spoke. Alex was elated, satisfied that the hours he'd spent
until now, listening either to silence or irrelevant conversations, had finally paid off.

He whispered, "Gotcha!" And if Lyle so much as
harmed a hair on Danithia's head, he'd wish he was never
born!

Chapter 11

Danithia and Ms. Griffin had an appointment to meet with one of the experts Danithia had carefully chosen to testify at trial. Dr. Putney's job was not only to tell the jurors about the extent of the injuries Ms. Griffin had suffered, but also convince them that Comex had maliciously, and with the specific intention to harm her and other people of African-American descent, induced them to partake in an experimental study before it was ready for human testing. He also would give them a detailed synopsis of what these harsh chemicals had done to her skin. Today, he would not only examine her, take tissue samples, but he would also take extensive photographs that would be blown up as exhibits for use in court.

After the intense, thorough examination, Dr. Putney ushered Patricia and Danithia into his private office, beautifully decorated in soft pastel shades.

"Please," he said, gesturing, "sit down."

Dr. Putney was a tall, gentle man with a quiet presence and, somewhat at odds with that gentleness, intense black eyes.

He cleared his throat. "I don't want to raise false hopes, but I wanted to advise both of you that the damage to the pigmentation and the skin might possibly be reversible."

"What!" Patricia cried.

"Really?" Danithia uttered.

He raised his palms to silence them. "This is my preliminary assessment of Ms. Griffin's condition. There are three major components to human skin, the epidermis, the dermis, and the subcutaneous. There are four layers of skin in the epidermis, the exception being the palms of your hands," he said, turning his own palms face out, "and the soles of the feet, which have five." Dr. Putney went into a lengthy and detailed dissertation on the human skin. Patricia and Danithia listened in silence with total concentration.

"So, you see," the doctor concluded, "it is quite possible that, unlike a normal burn, this chemical burn, may not have damaged the body's natural ability to restore itself if it is given some help, and those damaged cells are given a chance to breathe."

Patricia sat bolt upright. "What do you mean?"

"I suggest that we anesthetize you, scrape away those layers of dead skin, go through some intensive organic treatments to try to restore the natural pigmentation, and quite possibly we might be able to clear up this skin disorder."

"Will I look the same as I did before this happened?"

Danithia heard excitement and fear in Patricia's voice and reached over to gently hold her hand.

Dr. Putney said, "That will depend on many factors—some of which only time will tell. As for your nose, we can reconstruct it. I'm sure you realize that with the advancements in today's modern medicine, there's virtually nothing we cannot make, repair, or concoct. Your nasal passages are functional, all we need to do is rebuild the bridge."

Patricia sat back, stunned that it was possible for her to return to her former self.

"Now, let me warn you that chances are you'll still have the same deep pigmentation you had before, and since that seems to be the crux of the issue here, I thought I should forewarn you about this fact."

"I don't care about that. Not anymore."

"Your skin will be pink at first and brownish along the outer parameters. In fact, it will probably look very bad before it begins to look good and healthy."

"When can we get started?"

Danithia sat in silence. Although she was elated that Ms. Griffin might return to a semblance of her old self, she couldn't help but wonder if this would harm their case.

"Dr. Putney, with all due respect, and please don't misunderstand what I'm about to say, but doesn't this considerably alter our request for damages, especially if the damage can be reversed?"

"In my opinion, no. You see, this entire process will be, to say the least, costly. It will also be painful, cumbersome, burdensome, and it will be a long process. It also cannot be done in the United States. Ms. Griffin will have to accompany me to Europe."

"Why Europe?" Patricia asked.

"They have different medical guidelines and, for years, have incorporated natural medicine in their treatments. Also, France has developed a specialized surgery procedure we could utilize. It will delicately drain lymphatic fluids to reduce swelling, improve blood circulation, and it's an excellent way to eliminate pain. But of course, that would be only part of the intensive treatment you'll be receiving, Ms. Griffin."

He turned to Danithia. "To answer your question as it relates specifically to your case, all of these treatments should factor into damages. And, as I said earlier, since there is no guarantee it will work, that leads directly to your claim of additional pain and suffering."

He turned his full attention back to Patricia. "Please understand that what I'm telling you is my preliminary diagnosis. Obviously, I cannot determine for sure the depth of the damage until we begin the process. If more than the top two-to-four layers are damaged . . ."

"Then what?"

"The worst case scenario is that we'll scrape away the damaged skin only to find more destruction underneath. That's the gamble we'll be taking. But I feel it's worth the risk. At least you'll know you've tried."

"But my concern," Danithia interrupted, "is what will you tell the jury?"

"I'll describe in great detail what I believe the product did to Ms. Griffin's skin, how it managed to destroy her nose and render her hands arthritic and deformed. I'll also tell them of the possibility of restoration and at what cost, economically and personally."

"I'd rather not open up that door. That information we'll hold in reserve and reveal it only if the defendants ask."

"Oh, they'll ask."

"Why are you so sure of that?"

"Because, if they retain an expert of their own who's got any training in aesthetic medicine, once they examine her, in all probability they will reach the same conclusion I did."

"But, doctor," Patricia said. "I was under the impression that the treatment you described would not be known or readily available to a physician in this country."

"No, that's not what I said. You see, I've written many articles and have fought with the FDA to approve this treatment for various skin disorders in this country. If their expert reads his medical journals, and I'd venture to say that he does, he'll know about this possibility."

"Hmm," Danithia mumbled and wondered what this all meant. "Doctor, it would be extremely helpful to me if you could map out, step-by-step, this process and the cost for everything. And I need a fairly accurate estimate. Can you do that?"

"Of course. When would you like to have it?"

"As soon as possible."

"I can have it to you by week's end."

"Perfect."

Danithia turned to Patricia, who was noticeably quiet, and asked her if she had any more questions for the doctor, which she did. Danithia left the room to call Patrick and ask his opinion about settling for the twenty million dollars they had been offered. It seemed that an easy win, with a high monetary award, might not happen after all. Now, it was time for damage control.

On second thought, she would not phone. She would visit Patrick.

Chapter 12

It was very late by the time Danithia finally reached the hospital. The corridors were very quiet, only muted sounds from television programs could be heard from behind closed doors. She was a bit fearful that at any moment a nurse would appear and escort her out of the hospital, sternly admonishing her that it was past visiting hours. But she managed to make it to Room 457 without being detected. She paused briefly at Pat's door, wanting to knock but afraid that might arouse suspicion. She took a deep breath and pushed the door open.

Patrick's eyes opened immediately. He smiled when he realized it was Danithia and not another pesky nurse with a pill or thermometer.

"Danithia! What are you doing here?" His voice was stronger, his speech a little less slurred.

"I told you I would come see you, so here I am. I'm sorry to have come so late but I really must talk to you."

"What's going on?"

"I need your advice on the Comex case. Ms. Griffin and I went to see our expert today. And, well . . . he had some good news and, maybe, potentially bad news. Frankly, I'm not sure how to take it."

"What'd he say?"

"The good news is, he believes it quite possible that Patricia's injuries can be corrected. He said something about only the top layers of her skin being destroyed, but underneath there may very well be viable, healthy skin."

"Sounds wonderful. Now, tell me what are your concerns."

"In my opinion, this greatly minimizes our damages and the chance for a considerable monetary judgment. And we both know the only reason the firm has allowed me to stay on this case is because they're looking for that one-third they're going to get. Now, that may be a small amount."

"Juries are unpredictable, you can't begin to second-guess what they will or will not award."

"I know that. I know Ms. Griffin will be a very good witness, and her injuries support our claims. But if our own expert testifies that she can be repaired, then what will the jury think?"

"I don't know. What do you think they'll think?"

"That we're just a bunch of greedy lawyers chasing a large company for money, when that isn't the case at all. I mean, until today we didn't even know she could be fixed, but the jury won't know or care about that."

"It's your job to make them care about your client. Make a strong case that leaves them no doubt about the harm this product caused, prove to them that this malicious conduct was intentional and willful."

"Don't get me wrong, Pat. I know I have a strong case and I know I can prove everything you just said, but the fact of the matter is, the jury will probably be predominantly White, possibly disinterested in the things they'll surmise we choose to do to ourselves. And they'll probably care less about the damages."

Patrick chuckled. "I think you're selling us good White folks short."

"Pat, not everybody is like you. In my humble opinion there are very few people who care—I mean really care—about us. I don't want any of the plaintiffs to lose any more than they already have in this case."

"I get the feeling you've got something up your sleeve to remedy that."

She smiled. "You know me too well. Actually, what's been going through my head is the simple fact that, if we are successful and are awarded substantial monetary damages, the company will file for protection under bankruptcy and our plaintiffs will never see a dime."

"That's a possibility."

"They could also appeal the verdict, and that will discourage Ms. Griffin."

"You knew that before you took on the case. So, what's your point?"

She took a deep breath. "Chances are slim that we'll find all the victims—that they'll come forward with claims of their own. So what I've done is asked Dr. Putney—that's our expert—to give me some figures on how much the reconstructive surgery and facial treatments will run."

"Okay," Patrick said, encouragingly.

"Once I have those figures in my hands, I'd like to have one of our forensic attorneys run his own set of figures for approximately 10 to 20 plaintiffs, and then I'd like to take those numbers to Comex for settlement purposes."

"You don't want to go to trial? You want to settle out of court?" he asked, dumbfounded.

"If the circumstances were different, if the subject matter were not this explosive, and if I thought I could get together a large class of people to dangle before Comex, I wouldn't even think about settlement. But I know my people. And if they've allowed themselves to get involved in something like this, they're not going to come forward and risk the humiliation that will surely follow. Trust me on this. I know."

"You know?" Patrick said incredulously. "How do you know? By the fact that you're Black, that makes you know?"

She looked at him and saw the anger starting to build. She knew he didn't understand. He'd never believe that all Black people have some sort of innate understanding of each other's feelings. She had to tell him more.

"Pat, since you've been in the hospital I've been involved with a man named Alex. He's a security guard in our building."

Pat's eyebrows rose in a questioning way.

"He's not really a security guard and I can't tell you what it is he does—who he works for—but he's been chasing the perpetrators of this crime for quite some time."

"Oh really."

"Yes, and his involvement is a direct result of trying to track down wealthy African Americans who have disappeared, but they aren't dead and their families have not reported them as missing."

"They're victims too?"

"Yes."

"So that's where you get your profound insight."

"Yes," she said and smiled. "It's also because I'm Black that I know."

He grinned at her and said, "Touché! So . . . are we in love?"

"I'm definitely in something. Love?" She paused. "Maybe. I've never been in love before, so I can't say for sure."

"Now you're trying to pull my leg."

"No. I...it's just that—"

"You know the difference between lust and love?"

She raised her brow, "There's a thin line, I believe."

He chuckled. "Trust me it's not that thin, and you know the difference. Is he good to you?"

"I can't begin to tell you how much he's done for me, not only physically, but emotionally, mentally, spiritually."

"Sounds like a keeper."

"Only time will tell," she said wistfully. "But I will tell you this, I hope he'll be in my life for a very, very long time."

She sat quietly for a minute, thinking about Alex and how much she missed him at that very moment.

"I'm losing my train of thought and the reasons I sneaked in here. So, what do you think? Should I try this case—go all the way—or settle it and get what money I can?"

"I'd like to see you try it, for a number of reasons."

"And what might those reasons be?"

"For one, to show Lyle, Gerald, and Frank that you're a damn good lawyer."

"Thank you."

"And for two, there's a message that needs to be sent to people in this country, and the elements of this case teach such a lesson."

"And what lesson is that?"

"That color should not matter. And that trying to be something other than what you were born to be, is futile and leads to horrible situations like this one. Acceptance of the differences between us is necessary and if we don't stop making each other feel bad for those differences, we could all end up hurting ourselves even more."

"Pat—"

"What?"

"You're preaching."

"Right on, right on!" He raised his fist in a Black power salute.

"I'll think about it. Maybe the best thing to do is go to trial. I just don't want Ms. Griffin to lose."

"She won't lose. She has you, and you're a winner!"

Chapter 13

*B*ig, wet snowflakes whipped through the air, creating a cold, hostile world. Hazardous road conditions greeted the residents of Colorado each day, making drivers edgy and irritated long before they arrived at their destinations. And the heating bills skyrocketed high enough to kill any budget.

Danithia loved the snow, but once the full force of winter hit, she began to wish for spring. Even the thought of the upcoming holidays failed to cheer her because along with Christmas came the usual end of the fiscal year projects. Every year it was the same, and she was always surprised at how no one seemed to adequately prepare for the end-of-year drama, including herself. She shook her head in disbelief that so much had happened in just four months. Of course she was happy that her love affair with Alex was continuing. Actually, it was going very strong, and she enjoyed every single minute she spent with him, but sometimes this joy was overshadowed by the intricate details of her case against Comex.

She still had to make a decision. And she still did not know what course of action would be in her client's best interest. Patricia had issues that involved her self esteem, her image, her career, and the possibility of repair. Although repair would be a long, tedious, painful, not to mention uncertain process, it was something that lay within Patricia's reach, and she had to snatch it or live the rest of her life wondering if she had done the right thing. Monetary compensation was not beginning to cover what Patricia needed or wanted. But it was the only remedy the law allowed for her injuries, and that fact troubled Danithia. More than anything, she wished there was something else she could do.

Christmas! Danithia had avoided concentrating on Christmas. In fact, the idea of having to go shopping and fight monstrous crowds of rude, stressed-out people was more than she wanted to deal with right now, but everybody looked forward to receiving and giving presents, and she could not be an exception. She grabbed a notepad and began to scribble a list of gifts she wanted to purchase. A gift certificate for Valerie. A bottle of Patrick's favorite Cognac. For Patricia, a beautiful gold pen to urge her to begin to write again might be a perfect gift. And, of course, she had to come up with something extra special for her mother and father, maybe a four-day cruise to the Caribbean. She made a note for Valerie to look into that for her.

Then she thought about Alex. What item or items could she possibly purchase that would adequately express how she felt about him? That was going to be a tough one. She wrote his name and underlined it three times, adding several asterisks and question marks.

She contemplated these gifts and although it all sounded nice, she didn't feel the joy that should accompany the season, only a burdensome feeling of obligation. She sighed and chided herself for being so glum, but the simple fact was, she had a lot of things on her mind and Christmas was not one of them.

Later that evening as she prepared dinner for Alex and he attempted to put together a microwave utility cart, she looked up to find him staring at her.

"What?" she asked and stopped stirring the spaghetti sauce.

"What's wrong, babe? You seem down."

"I'm okay, just tired I guess."

"Do you want me to finish dinner? I can do this later."

"No, I got it."

But Alex noticed that she still just held the spoon in her hand and was no longer twirling it around the reddish, fragrant mixture. He approached her, clasped his hands around her waist, and she leaned into him, resting her head upon his chest.

"What do you want for Christmas?" she asked.

"Nothing."

She turned around, laced her fingers around his neck, and lightly kissed his lips.

"Nothing?"

"Well, maybe a little more of that." He kissed her back, deeply, meaningfully.

Then she started to cry.

"Baby, what's going on? Why are you crying?"

"I don't know," she wailed. "I really, really don't. I've been feeling emotional and weird all day."

"Come on," he said and led her to the sofa. "Lie down. You want something to drink?"

"Maybe a glass of wine."

"Coming right up. You rest, babe."

He hurried to the kitchen, his steps quick and urgent. For reasons he didn't quite understand, he felt panicked. She had never acted like this before. Even when she lost her dog Tanya, she didn't seem this overwhelmed with sadness. He fumbled around in the kitchen, searching for the cork screw, then it seemed to take forever to decide which wine to open. He opened and closed cabinet doors until he finally found the crystal wine goblets she loved, rinsed them out, and then struggled with the cork, breaking it in half before it was fully ejected. He cursed silently because now it was going to be a bear trying to get the remainder of the cork out without breaking it into small pieces. He hated to see small specks of brown cork floating in his favorite Cabernet.

"Here you go," he said and was amazed that, when he finally approached her, she was fast asleep, snoring lightly. He watched the swell of her breasts as her chest rose and fell rhythmically with each breath she took. Her nostrils flared ever so slightly, and a hoarse, rough noise followed each exhale. He loved this woman, everything about her, even the fact that she snored. To him it was cute. He placed the wine glasses on the coffee table and sat on the floor at her feet, just watching her.

After about an hour, she awoke and the first thing she saw was Alex, sipping wine and smiling.

"Hey," he said.

"Hey yourself." She stretched and yawned, finally pulling herself to a sitting position. "I can't believe I fell asleep like that. What time is it?"

"Nine o'clock."

"Nine o'clock!" she exclaimed. "Why'd you let me sleep so long?"

"Because you needed it."

"But Alex, dinner's probably ruined. Did you turn the sauce off?"

"Yes I did. Everything's fine. I finished up dinner while you slept. You still want a glass of wine?"

"Yeah, yeah I do." She raised the glass to her lips and gagged at the smell of it. Suddenly, she was on her feet, running to the bathroom.

Alex followed quickly on her heels, but she slammed the door in his face. He could hear her retching and gagging behind the closed door. Then, finally, the toilet flushed and water started running as she rinsed her mouth, spitting repeatedly in the sink.

"I'm okay," she said when she finally emerged with a light sheen of sweat on her forehead.

He stroked her brow expecting to feel skin that was feverish and clammy, but it wasn't.

"Do I have a fever?" she asked with closed eyes, relishing his gentle, loving touch on her face.

"Nope. You feel any better now?"

"Yeah. I guess I ate something that didn't agree with me. What does food poisoning feel like?"

"Severe stomach cramps, nausea, vomiting, dizziness. Besides the vomiting, do you have any of these other symptoms?"

"No, I feel fine. Just wanna lie down again. Alex, do you mind if I just call it a night and go to bed?"

"You go ahead, babe. I'm going to finish up that utility cart."

"Okay," she said, again seeming very lethargic as she crept down the hallway, then softly closing the bedroom door behind her.

~ ~ ~

It was Saturday afternoon before she began to stir. Sounds and smells of Alex preparing eggs and bacon finally reached her, shaking her from her unconscious state. She glanced at the clock, blinked several times, it could not be this late.

"Alex!" she shrieked.

He heard her loud voice. Alarmed, he ran to her.

"What?"

"Is it really twelve-fifteen?"

"You scared me to death hollering like that," he said both alarmed and annoyed. "Yes, it's twelve-fifteen, why? Did you have somewhere to be today?"

"No, it's just that . . ." Puzzled, almost fearful, she looked around the room. "I never sleep this late, Alex, you know that. What's wrong with me?"

"It's not a crime to sleep late on a Saturday, Miss Lawyer. Relax, enjoy your day off."

"That's not it, Alex. I'm not feeling like myself. I think something's wrong with me."

"Because you threw up and slept late?"

"Yes! That and because, well, I just don't feel right. I feel damn near catatonic, and I'm so bitchy." She paused, wrinkled her nose and sniffed. "What are you cooking? It smells—ugh."

"Bacon and eggs. Since when can't you identify the scent of bacon? Or not like it?"

"See what I mean! Oh, God, what is wrong with me?" she shrieked, holding her face in her hands.

He gently pulled her hands from her face and hoped she wouldn't get mad at him for what he was about to say.

"Danithia? Are you on your period?"

"Why does everything have to be about me and my period? Huh?" she shouted. "That's all men ever think, it's your period, it's your period," she said, turning her head from side to side and using a mocking tone of voice.

He watched her with growing fascination and began to agree with her, because she definitely wasn't herself.

"Do you wanna fight?" he asked her in a mild tone.

"No, I'm not trying to pick a fight. Oh, just forget it!" She said, tossing the blankets aside, practically running to the bathroom.

She tried to slam the door, but it just swished and silently closed.

"Damn door won't even slam!" she screamed and lowered herself to the toilet. She sat there fighting tears, wondering what the hell was going on. And as she began to wipe herself she glanced at the tissue and wondered when was the last time she'd seen crimson there. And as quickly as a stiff, cold Colorado wind will mess up even the best hairstyle, it hit her.

"I'm pregnant."

She stayed in the bathroom, staring at her reflection in the mirror for a long, long time. She lifted her nightgown and studied her body. Did she see any evidence? Not really. She turned left and then right, examining her abdomen, and it looked the same to her. She did notice that her breasts seemed swollen, and they were definitely tender to the touch, but that didn't seem all that unusual. It happened from time to time, particularly if she were about to start her period. Then she tried to calculate in her head the last time she'd been visited by the so-called "curse," and could not recall when.

She filled the bathtub with warm water and lots of fragrant bubbles. She needed to relax and think.

"Hey babe?" she heard Alex's muffled, questioning voice through the door.

"What?"

"Are you okay now?"

"Come in."

"Is it safe for me, or should I go get my boxing gloves out?"

She laughed. "Go get 'em, then come in."

He opened the door and she blew a handful of bubbles at him.

"Sorry for acting such a fool."

"What's up, babe?"

"You will not believe what I think is going on."

"Try me."

"First, join me."

"With or without clothes?" he asked.

"Umm, let me think." She made him wait about thirty seconds before she replied. "Without!"

He undressed very quickly and slipped in at the opposite end. He cradled her ankle in the palm of his hand and massaged the bottom of her foot with soothing strokes.

Danithia closed her eyes, enjoying this sensual foot massage, while her mind reeled at the fact that she could be pregnant. How should she tell him? She wondered how he'd react, and if he'd be angry with her for allowing such a thing to happen.

"So" Alex said, interrupting her thoughts, "When do you think the baby's due?"

Her eyes flew open, and she jerked her foot away so quickly that she slightly grazed him in a most delicate spot.

"Ow!" he howled.

"I'm sorry. What did you just say?" she stammered.

"You heard me. Damn, Danithia that hurt. You keep that up and this will be the only kid we ever have."

She watched him cradle himself, his face attempting to mask pain, replacing it with joy.

"How'd you know?"

"Danithia, believe it or not, but you are not the first woman I've been with. Remember, my ex-wife?"

"Yeah, but I thought you told me you didn't have any children."

He looked down, then up at her. "I don't, but I remember the symptoms."

"She was pregnant? What happened?"

"Miscarriage in her third month. She was so devastated that she never wanted to try again."

Danithia unconsciously placed her hand across her belly. Cold shivers of goose bumps raced up her arms.

"She'd had a hard childhood. Lots of terrible things happened to her, including abuse by one of her uncles. I tried as hard as I could to make things right for her, but I could never quite reach her mind. No matter how much I loved her, she never seemed to fully reciprocate."

"Alex, you've never really talked to me about her—about your relationship with her."

"It's not an easy thing to discuss. And please don't get me wrong when I say this, but I really didn't want to have children with her. I was scared that she would be incapable of loving a child the way it deserves to be loved. You know what I mean?"

"Yes, I think I do."

"She had trouble loving herself. I realized that later, after everything was over. So I wondered if she would have made a good mother. Maybe God made the choice for both of us and decided that having a child wasn't a good thing."

"Do you really think God makes those kinds of decisions? I mean, can't it have just been that something was wrong with the fetus? Nothing more, nothing less?"

"Could be. Who knows for sure. What you believe God is or is not responsible for is an individual thing. Shoot, at times I waver back and forth on how I feel about the so-called Almighty Being, that great spiritual force that shapes our lives."

She watched him with growing amazement and renewed respect for him as a man—as her man.

"Alex?"

"Hmm?"

"What kind of mother do you think I'll make?"

He shook his head and stared at her. Finally, he smiled. "Fabulous."

"Really?"

"Wonderful, insightful, a great teacher, patient, loving, kind. I could go on and on, but I think besides your belly swelling, your head will too."

He touched her stomach, placing his palm against her taut, smooth brown skin. He splayed his fingers open and his hand almost covered the entire surface of it. Suddenly, he threw his head back and yelled, "I'm going to be a d-a-d-d-y!" He splashed water, scooped up a handful of bubbles and blew them at her. He stood up and pulled her to her feet.

He was silly with excitement, and she hated to burst his enthusiasm with a reality he needed to face. "Alex, it's not certain yet that I'm pregnant."

"Oh, you're pregnant. How else would you explain the way you've been acting? Hmm, answer me that."

She had to chuckle. "Let's find out for sure."

"Get some clothes on, girl, we're going to the drug store."

"I want to make love first. Do you think it would hurt the baby, if there is a baby?"

He didn't say a word, just shook his head back and forth. "Probably not if we do it like this."

He pulled the shower curtain closed, unplugged the drain, turned on the shower, rinsing all the suds from her body, running his hand softly over the curve and swell of her breasts. He cupped them, then, with water hitting the back of his head, began to suckle one. The soft, gentle pressure of his tongue against her sensitive nipple caused her to arch back. Moaning softly, she grasped his head and held him firmly, not wanting him to ever stop. His hand trailed down her side, her thigh, then settled against her mound of soft curls. He touched her most sensitive spot, stroking it, teasing it, until she began to murmur his name over and over. And, as usual, the earth seemed to move with each gyration of her hips. Tremors and strong pulsations began deep within her. Alex had to literally hold her up as ecstasy swept her away.

~ ~ ~

With growing excitement building between them from the time they left the house, to the checkout line at the grocery store, and even in the car on the way back home, they talked in excited tones, wondered if it was a boy or a girl, what they would name it, and how they would raise it. She was determined that, if the child was a girl, she would raise her to be strong and independent, but also teach her a delicate balance of how to be dependent and somewhat needy, so a man could feel secure in his role as a caretaker and provider. Alex wanted what he called a "little man," so he could teach him all about the important things in life like sports, politics, and of course the art of loving and understanding a woman. Although that, he admitted, would be the toughest lesson of all to teach. Danithia punched him in the arm declaring that it was not all that hard to love a woman, and he just laughed until tears streamed down his face.

She hurried into the bathroom, and for the second time that day, slammed the door in his face, declaring that she needed privacy. He stubbornly stood at its entrance, tapping his foot.

"It's positive." she mumbled.

"What? What did you say, I can't hear you."

"It's positive!"

He burst into the tiny room. "It is? It is!"

"Look! The instructions said if the color changes, it's positive. It's blue."

He stared at the small vial until Danithia thought he was perhaps frozen with shock. She watched his face change, and when he looked at her, she saw tears forming in his eyes.

"We're going to be parents, Danithia."

She brushed away the tear that had started to trickle down his cheek. "Yeah, I know."

"I love you with all my heart. You know that, don't you?"

"That's the one thing I do know for sure."

He embraced her with a fierce hug of protection and affection and happiness.

She clung to him as he rocked her back and forth, matching the turmoil she felt inside. Her emotions a see-saw, swinging high and low, so much so that she did not know what to do, how to feel, what to say. How was she supposed to feel? They weren't even married, yet she was carrying his child. How was she supposed to address the sensitive issue of marriage with Alex when it was something they rarely discussed? And, did she want to be his wife? Did she truly want to make that kind of lifetime commitment to him? Was she even ready? And, oh God, what would her parents say? While her mind conducted this silent battle she never uttered a single word about her fears. She simply held him, letting the warmth of his body comfort her.

"Danithia? Every year my family celebrates Kwanzaa. I want us, you and me, to be a part of that. We've got a lot to celebrate and I think it'd be appropriate to share our joy with family."

Her stomach tumbled, she hadn't even thought of his parents' reaction to all this. A moan escaped her and she began to tremble.

"What...what is it, Danithia?

"I'm— I'm—" she stammered.

"What, babe? Here, sit down."

"Alex, what will your parents think of me?" she shrieked. "I mean it's not like I'm some naive teenager unaware of birth control! How did this happen?"

Alex watched her beautiful face become a mask of embarrassment and uncertainty. He took both of her hands inside his and forced her to look into his eyes.

"First of all, birth control is a two-way street. You knew it and I knew it. Second, my parents will love and accept you and our child because I love you. And third . . ." he paused as he reached to pull her onto his lap. "Now, third,—no, no, wait. Before I continue with my third point, I need to ask you a question?"

Danithia held her breath hoping she already knew what he was going to say.

"Babe, how do you feel about all this—I mean really— now that we're no longer fantasizing, now that the baby is a reality, are you still excited and happy?"

She didn't immediately respond, she gazed at the floor and struggled for the right words to come.

Alex waited.

"It seems like all my adult life I've fallen in and out of love with various men. Sometimes the pain from ending a relationship would make me not want to go on—to try to love someone again.

"Then, you came along in an unexpected form—a wanna-be security officer," she said and chuckled. "And since the day you rescued me in that parking garage, it seems my life has not been the same."

"Is that a good or bad thing, Danithia?"

"It's neither good nor bad—it is what I've dreamed of— exactly the kind of relationship I would dream about after my latest love became my ex-love. Alex, I didn't know it until now but you are what I've always wanted, the kind of man I would never have imagined would enter and stay in my life." She paused to kiss his lips.

"Alex," she continued, "promise me that this baby will have your sexy lips."

"Promise me it'll have your pretty brown eyes," he replied.

"It's got to have your sense of humor and sensitivity," she added.

"And your intelligence and, if it's a girl, let her inherit your sexy walk and these beautiful legs!"

They laughed and hugged and rejoiced that soon baby would make them three!

~ ~ ~

They had a lovely Christmas with Danithia's family, then on the 30th of December, they flew to Chicago. During the flight, Alex explained more to her about sharing in the spiritual holiday of Kwanzaa. In a strong voice, filled with pride, he told her about the origin of Kwanzaa.

"In 1966, a Dr. Karenga from San Diego developed the concept for this type of celebration, realizing that all other cultures had a holiday, but African Americans did not. So, in recognition of our heritage, struggle, and survival, he thought that a celebration of our strengths should begin.

"He wanted us to give thanks for the blessings of a new year, for families to come together with new resolutions, reassessments, reclaiming and recommitting to the seven principles that are the basis for Kwanzaa.

Danithia listened with fascination. "What seven principles, Alex?"

"Unity; self-determination; collective works; cooperative economics; purpose; creativity and faith. The Swahili word for unity is "Umoja," he said, his voice rising as his excitement began to build.

"Danithia, I want our child—our family—to be one that exudes positive Black self-esteem and spirituality. How do you feel about that?"

"It sounds good to me. I just need to educate myself more about this celebration so we can incorporate it in our lives and do it the right way."

"Wait till you see my parents' home. That'll show you what we need to do next year."

She looked at him "You're predicting our future?"

"Without you in it, there is no future for me." He leaned toward her and kissed her.

"I love you, Alex."

He continued to educate her about Kwanzaa, now using the Swahili names for the seven principles, which she dutifully repeated, stumbling over them at first. He spoke to her with a quiet passion. His voice soothed her, and before she knew it, the swaying motion of the plane had lulled her to sleep.

~ ~ ~

"There's my father. Hey, dad!" Alex shouted and waved his muscular arms like an excited child.

"It's good to see you, son." Mr. Powers embraced him warmly. "Young lady," he said over Alex's shoulder, "you're much prettier than Alex described."

"Thank you." She felt welcomed, yet a bit embarrassed.

"Your mother's arthritic hip is acting up today, she's sitting over there." Mr. Powers pointed to a smartly dressed woman, whose smile lit up her entire face.

"There's my girl!" Alex rushed to her side. He hugged her so long, Danithia thought he might be crying or something.

When he finally released his mother, she immediately came over to give Danithia and warm embrace.

"Welcome to the family," she whispered, then took Danithia's hand and pulled her away. "I can't wait to hear all about you."

Danithia risked a glance over her shoulder, but Alex and his father were engaged in deep conversation. The two men so closely resembled each other that watching them was like glancing at a mirror reflecting present and future. She could see Alex thirty years from now, still handsome, still strong, and hopefully still in love with her.

~ ~ ~

Alex's parents still lived in the home he was raised in, a modest house with four bedrooms and a large family room, which, Alex explained, had been added by converting the garage. The minute Danithia entered this house, she was enveloped with a kind of warmth that was indescribable. The sights, sounds, and smells were so comfortable, so genuine, that she immediately felt at home and among family.

They entered the family room and Danithia found an interesting collection of various items on the floor.

"The symbols of Kwanzaa." Alex came up behind her and cradled her in his arms.

"Really!"

"Yep. First you put down a straw mat, then you put the candelabrum in the center. You want seven candles—for the seven principles."

"Okay, the seven principles you told me about on the plane."

"Right. Now you put ears of corn on both sides of the mat. In our house we have three children, so there are three ears of corn."

He pointed to the other items. "These gifts are hand-made. This is the unity cup, and this is soil from our back-

yard. And you top it all off with a basket of fruit." He
paused. "You know what this is, right?"

"Of course I do. It's the black flag. And I know what
the colors stand for."

"What?" he questioned teasingly.

"Red stands for the blood . . ."

"Or struggle, right."

"Green stands for the land . . ."

"Our hope. . . our future."

"And black stands for the color of our skin."

"Yeah, our race."

"See, I told you I knew."

"In the Kwanzaa celebration, we light one candle each
day in honor of that day's principle, the black one first. It
is the Unity candle." He pointed to the red candle on its
right. "This was lit on the second day, the day we acknowledge self-determination. On the third day, we light the
green one, representing collective work and responsibility."

She listened and watched him with fascination.

He said, "On the fourth day, another red candle. It's
the day we emphasize patronizing our Black-owned businesses. Tonight, my parents will light this green one."

"What's the principle today?"

"Today is purpose, or Nia. Tomorrow is Kuumba, or
creativity. It's the day when we acknowledge and celebrate our creative side. Sometimes we make gifts, but we
don't give them to each other until the seventh day."

"Is that principle, giving?"

"No, it's called "Imani" or faith. And on that day I'll
present something very special to you."

She smiled and hugged him. Like an excited child, she
asked "What is it? Huh? Tell me what did you get me?
Tell me!"

"You'll see. All I'll tell you about your gift is that it will be in accordance with that day's principle, it will be a gift given from the heart. We'll celebrate with a huge dinner. Oh, I forgot to tell you something important."

"What?"

"During Kwanzaa, you're supposed to fast for a week from sunrise to sunset."

"Why?"

"To cleanse the body, discipline the mind, and uplift the spirit. But I already told my parents that you couldn't fast."

"What reason did you give them?"

"None. I just said you couldn't, that you have to eat."

"Alex, are you going to tell them I'm pregnant?"

"Danithia, baby, let me explain something to you about my relationship with my parents and my brother and sister."

He took her by the hand and led her to the flowered deep- cushioned sofa.

"I'm very open and honest with my parents about almost everything. For the most part, the only exception is my job. I can't tell them what I'm working on, but other than that, I don't lie or hide anything from them."

"I'm not asking you to lie. I just . . ." She sighed and threw her hands up in the air.

"What, Danithia? You just what?"

"I'm uncomfortable, okay? I mean, what in the world are they going to think of me, a grown professional woman, pregnant like some teenager who doesn't know a thing about birth control."

He could see she was agitated, so he scooted her into his lap.

"Babe, it's not like that. I thought we already had this discussion. First of all, my parents are not judgmental, so don't worry about that. Second, I'm totally in love with you, and they know that."

Her eyes filled with tears, which touched his heart.

"Remember the principle for day seven?"

"Yes." she sniffled. "Faith."

"Have faith, babe, have faith. Everything's going to be all right. And I do mean, everything."

~ ~ ~

Every day was full of excitement and discoveries for her. She met the rest of the Powers clan, and was again instantly enveloped with love and kindness from Alex's brother, Seth, and his sister, Adrionna.

While the rest of the world celebrated New Year's Eve, they were in the kitchen baking cookies and cakes from scratch, learned certain terms in Swahili, and got to know each other. Adrionna and Danithia were only two years apart, so they had much in common, and they laughed and teased each other as if they'd known each other all their lives.

That evening, they enjoyed the Karamu Feast with gift exchange, affirmations, and a solemn moment of reflection on the new year's goals. Joyfully, the family reaffirmed their love and commitment to one another.

Music could be heard from every room in the house, the rhythmic beat of African drums and cymbals or Reggae music. And they danced. Alex and Adrionna performed an African dance twirling and clapping in unison, or shouting Swahili words. The family gathered around them, clapping and encouraging them. Danithia swayed and bopped to the beat, completely engrossed in the power of their collective love, of this spiritual celebration. Never before had she thought it possible to praise Blackness in this manner. Many, many times she wished that Patricia were here to

participate so she too could revel in the beauty of simply
being Black!

~ ~ ~

The entire family was called to the family room on January
1st. Mr. Powers, dressed in African attire, stood before the
family and held a bowl of water high in the air before pour-
ing a small amount on the floor.

He threw back his head and shouted. "This libation is
being poured out in honor of our ancestors. Habari!
Greetings to my family!"

In unison, everyone replied, "Greetings!"

"Today, is the final day of our Kwanzaa celebration.
And we join together in the wisdom and honor of Imani—
faith. I'm going to deviate from our usual proceedings, to
allow my eldest son, Lewis Alexander Powers, to take the
floor."

He stepped aside, and Alex came forward.

Alex stood before everyone, and Danithia noticed that
he seemed nervous, not as self-assured as she'd always
known him to be, and this frightened her.

"Greetings!" he began. "Today I stand before all the
people I love to not only reaffirm my love to all of you but
also to declare a special, most powerful love for someone
new."

Everyone looked at Danithia, and even though she was
so proud of him at that moment, she wanted to slink away.
She wasn't used to this kind of attention.

"For almost forty years this man and woman," he said,
pointing to his parents, "have loved each other for better,
for worse, for richer and poorer. And we've seen some
poor times."

Everyone laughed and shook their head in agreement.

"But through it all, they have stuck together. From the
birth of their first child—yours truly," he said grinning, "to

the second child, that beautiful woman I am proud to call my sister, to the baby of this family, Seth, they have continued to love and provide all of us with the kind of support that I believe is unparalleled.

"I have watched this man and woman," Alex said, kneeling before them. "Together they have taught me so much. And for that I say thank you."

He got off his knees, walked over to Danithia and knelt before her.

"I want forty-plus years with you. I want to rise each day and know you're there loving me, caring for me, and I will do the same for you."

Danithia struggled to maintain her composure, but tears started to form anyway.

"I want the moon to never come out or the stars to sprinkle the nighttime sky with you and me in an angry state of mind. I want our babies to know love, and I want them to know understanding and compassion. I want them to know respect, and I want them to love you as I do. I never, ever, want to experience life alone. I want to always be with you. Please be my lady—my wife—my 'mkewe'."

"What's that mean?" she said, and everyone smiled.

"It's Swahili for wife or life partner.

"Oh," she said, her heart warming.

"Will you have me, trust me, respect me? Be my best friend, my confidante, my companion, my spiritual partner? And will you allow me to be the one you love until death takes one of us?"

The room was quiet while her eyes were on him, and him alone. She knelt before him and whispered, "If I could wish for anything, anything in this vast, huge world, it would be that death would never rear its ugly head and take me away from you. You're already my friend—my best friend. And you're the man I want to grow old with.

The baby I carry deep within me will be one of the lucki-
est children alive because you are its daddy."

Just then a man came into the room. He walked up to
both Alex and Danithia.

Alex stood and the two men embraced. Danithia
looked from one to the other and couldn't figure out this
rude interruption.

"So," Alex said and grasped her hand. "Was that a
'yes'?"

She nodded her head, confirming her decision, and the
room erupted with clapping, hoops and hollers, congratu-
lations, and excitement.

"Your timing was just a little off, Reverend," Alex said.

"You're a pastor," Danithia exclaimed.

"Yes, and if you're willing, today you can become man
and wife. Right here, right now."

"Today!"

"Your future is in this room. It can begin now." The
Reverend said.

"But what about my parents, my friends?"

"We're here," she heard her mother's voice.

"Mommy!" she squealed, and before she could reach
her mother, in came her father, Valerie, Patrick in a wheel
chair, and Patricia Griffin.

"Ohhh, my God. You're all here. Alex, how did you
do this?"

"Girlfriend," Valerie spoke up, "he chartered a plane,
and we all came together."

"You chartered a plane!" she echoed, surprised.

"A company plane, Danithia."

The Reverend spoke again. "Now, can we proceed?"

She looked around, at all the expectant faces, but
before she could answer, her mother stepped forward.

"There's one more thing she needs before this can begin."

Adrionna came into the room holding the most exquisite wedding gown Danithia had ever seen.

"Ohhhhh, you guys . . ." She pressed her hands to her face in speechless surprise.

Alex and his family began to chant, "Imani, Imani, Imani! over and over again, then "Faith, Faith, Faith!"

Danithia's mother raised a hand to silence them. She walked up to her only daughter and took her hands.

"Do you love him?"

"Yes, Momma, with all my heart."

"Do you want to marry him?"

"Yes."

"Are you mentally, physically, spiritually, and emotionally ready to make that commitment now?"

"Yes."

"Then I'll help you get dressed."

Once again, the room erupted in celebratory shouts of praise, thanks, and joy.

Danithia walked up to Patrick and kissed his cheek. She embraced Patricia. "I can't tell you how many times I've thought about you."

"Why were you thinking of me? Because of Kwanzaa?"

"Well, yes. How did you know?"

"Your young man told me that he hoped you'd marry him on the last day of Kwanzaa. And after he told me a little about Kwanzaa and all it stands for, I did some research. And it was then I knew this was the kind of celebration I've needed all my life."

"Hey!" Danithia heard her mother say. "Are you planning on getting married today, or what?"

"Today!" She hurried off with her mother, Alex's sister, and Valerie at her side. Valerie would be the maid of honor, and Seth would be the best man. Her bouquet was made up of African violets, pink tulips and baby's breath. She knew the tulips were out of season, so someone had gone to a lot of trouble to make them available for her today. She thought about Alex, down on his knees, proposing, and her stomach fluttered with excitement. She knew he could be very romantic, but this was totally unexpected.

"Who picked the dress?" she asked her mother.

"Alex did."

She looked from her mother to his sister, "Without any help from either of you guys?"

"We'll never tell," both women said in unison.

"Whoever selected it, it's beautiful. I love the color, and these tiny pearls. I couldn't have done a better job myself."

"Well, let's hope it fits."

She tried it on and it was perfect. "I can't believe it!" She exclaimed.

"Alex had the seamstress use a pair of your favorite slacks to get your waist size and the length. That's a smart man you're marrying."

"Yeah he's smart. I just wish I could say the same thing about myself."

"What you talkin' about, girl?" her mother asked.

"Momma, do you know about the baby?"

"I knew the day after you did. Alex came to see us, asked for your hand in marriage, and he was very careful to explain that your being pregnant had nothing to do with his proposal. It may have pushed it up a bit, but it had been his intention for some time to marry you."

"I didn't know. I mean I hoped, but I didn't know for sure. We've skimmed the subject, but that was all."

"He said you seemed a bit skittish about marriage, that you'd run from the subject whenever it came up."

"I didn't realize I was doing that. Maybe I was afraid to address it 'cause I didn't know if he wanted to go down that road again."

When Danithia was dressed, except for the veil, Valerie joined them with her camera. She snapped picture after picture as mother and daughter pinned the veil, a ritual as sacred as the father escorting the daughter down the aisle.

"You're so beautiful. Oh God, I can't believe it. My baby's finally gettin' married!" Her mother wiped her eyes, then rummaged in her handbag. "I brought something with me. Now, where is it?"

"What is it, Momma? I'm ready to get married now."

"Remember, in college you took that creative writing class? You wrote a poem that was so beautiful I wanted you to read it again."

"Which poem are you talking about, Momma?"

"Infinity."

Danithia took the folded piece of paper from her mother's hand, and with every stanza she read she knew exactly why her mother had given it to her at this time. When she finished reading, she was no longer nervous or afraid.

~ ~ ~

Danithia took a deep breath, held her head high, gathered the train in one hand, and clasped her waiting father's in the other. And with that, the ceremony could begin.

The wedding song began to play as soon as Danithia appeared. Alex watched her walking towards him, admiring for the thousandth time her regal air, straight back, erect posture, and he was so proud that today this woman would become his wife.

"Here comes my best friend," he whispered to Seth.

"Dearly beloved ..." The reverend began the age-old marriage ceremony, and once the vows had been spoken, he added, "Is there anything either of you would like to say to the other?"

Alex smiled at Danithia, his eyes bright, brimming with tears.

"I would," she said. She unfolded the piece of paper tucked inside her glove.

"Alex, I didn't realize until today that all my life I've loved you. Even when I didn't know you, I loved you. My mother reminded me today that everything I ever wanted, everything I ever dreamed about, I have with you.

"I wrote a poem a long time ago, but until now I didn't know I was talking about you. May I read it?"

Alex was so overcome with emotion that all he could do was nod his head.

"I hear your voice and my heart begins to sing
Sweet words and melodies of love that
Croon ever so softly in my ear,
Whispering three beautiful words, 'I love you.'

"Your touch sets my skin afire,
I fan the flames of desire
that causes my heart to flutter.
I feel so very, very weak,
I start to ache and
My soul softly surrenders to whatever it is you want me
    to do.

"If I could tuck your essence away and
neatly stash it beneath my arm and gently
    carry it with me,
Oh, I surely would,

To hold forever dear and close.

"For the depth of love I have for you
reaches to the bottom of the deepest sea,
Expands beyond the heavens to whatever lies on the
    other side,
And it is as wide as the very universe.

"'Cause my love for you my dear sweet Alex, is
Infinity times infinity times infinity."

Unable to contain her tears, she looked up at him as he brushed away tears and cleared his throat. She could hear others softly weeping, noses being blown, and to her surprise the pastor too was overcome with emotion.

"Wow. I guess after something like that, all I can say is I now pronounce you man and wife. What God has joined together, let no man ever pull apart. You may kiss your bride."

With a trembling hand, Alex lifted her veil, stared into her eyes, cradled her face in the palms of his hands, and then with the softest, purest motion, swept his lips back and forth over hers, whispering, "I love you. I love you. I love you."

Chapter 14

It was a new year. Danithia and Alex had taken their love to a new level, and to top things off, they had a baby on the way. Danithia was overcome with all of this when she returned to her office and found a new name plate on her door. Danithia R. Powers. Wow! In only seven months, her life had changed so much. It was incredible, almost unbelievable, but everything was true, and she was happy—truly happy for the first time in her life.

Mountains of work awaited her, but she separated everything into piles, noting priority. She could handle it. She would not let the demands of this job hurt her or her unborn child.

After wading through all the mail, she turned to her faxes. She stopped short when she saw one from Peter Ivy. Comex's attorneys had made another settlement offer. Thirty million per known plaintiff! Close, she thought, they're getting closer.

It was time to call Patricia. She hadn't spoken with her since the day after the wedding, when Patricia, Valerie, Pat, and her parents had left Chicago, leaving her to enjoy a miniature honeymoon.

"Patricia, hi, this is Danithia."

"Hello. And how is the newlywed and best lawyer in Colorado?"

Danithia chuckled. "I'm wonderful, thank you. And how are you doing?"

"I'm blessed."

"I just got back to the office, and while I was gone we had another settlement offer from Comex."

"How much?"

"Thirty million per known plaintiff."

"What do you think? Should we settle?"

"At this point, it's not a bad idea. Let me tell you why. I strongly believe we'll win this case and a jury will award us huge damages, compensatory and punitive."

"Great, then let's decline."

"But," Danithia continued, "I also know that often the defendant corporation will file for protection under the bankruptcy act, and we'll never see a dime. If we settle before a jury can award lots of money, we'll have a better chance of collecting."

"It's not the money I want, Danithia. You know that."

"I know, but as I've explained before, it's really the only viable remedy we have under the law."

"I want them shut down! Danithia, I want them out of business!"

"I know, I know. Patricia, please understand that while I believe that might happen, there's also a possibility that it might not."

"Do you think they've upped the ante because they're afraid of us?"

"It's possible. But the way litigation works, offering a settlement is not necessarily indicative of fear. Sometimes companies offer to settle simply to rid themselves of what they might consider a 'nuisance' lawsuit."

"You believe they think I'm a nuisance?"

"No. That's not what I'm saying at all. Settlement offers happen in almost every case. Before a judge, it's considered a good faith effort to stop the high cost of litigation. It's actually a pretty standard practice."

"Danithia, I don't know. You make this whole litigation thing seem so ordinary and commonplace, and I'm getting so tired of all of this. I just want it over."

"Please, Patricia, don't misunderstand me. I am willing to fight for you, and nothing about this case is ordinary or simple. I'm just trying to explain the process, and I guess I'm doing an awful job."

"Don't beat yourself up, child. Like I said, I'm just tired. I want to move on to other things, yet I feel stuck here, dealing with this mess."

"Patricia, do you want me to accept the settlement offer?"

"No...yes...oh, I don't know."

Danithia frowned at the Comex fax in her hand. "I'll tell you what I think we should do. Let me prepare a counteroffer of perhaps forty million for twenty plaintiffs, known and unknown, with payment due at the time the settlement agreement is signed. You'll receive your portion, minus attorneys' fees and costs. The rest of the money would then go into a trust fund for those people we haven't yet identified; and this matter will be considered over, at least as far as you're concerned."

"I was violated, horribly violated, and I can't believe they can just hand me and anybody else a lousy twenty, thirty, or even forty million dollars while they get away scot-free! That just doesn't seem right."

"It's our only remedy under the law, Patricia."

"It's not enough. I'm sorry Danithia, but it's just not enough!"

~ ~ ~

Midnight. Gerald Primes left his office after a particularly grueling day of trial preparation. Alex had waited patiently for him to appear. He found it uncanny how this man totally resembled his whiny voice, reminding him of a sneaky weasel. Alex approached him.

"Gerald Primes?"

Startled, Gerald looked up at the bulky figure. Immediately, he raised his hands. "I don't have any cash on me!"

"Are you Gerald Primes?" Alex demanded.

"Yes...yes, I am. Why?"

Alex presented his badge. "You're under arrest for attempted murder, conspiracy to commit murder, breaking and entering, and destruction of private property."

In the fluorescent light of the garage, Gerald's face looked almost green. "What! "What in the world are you talking about?"

"Please place your hands behind your back."

"I most certainly will not! What do you think you're doing? Why in the world am I being accused of attempted murder?"

Swiftly, expertly, Alex had the man in handcuffs. "You have the right to remain silent. Anything you say, can and will be used against you in a court of law. You have the right to retain an attorney. If you cannot afford one, one will be provided for you."

"I am an attorney." Gerald Primes shouted. "For god's sake, you've got the wrong man."

"No, sir. I believe I have the right man. In fact, I have a taped conversation between yourself, Lyle McGregor, and Franklin Ditz, that will prove I definitely have the right man. Now, please come with me."

Primes started to protest, his shock was so great that there was nothing he could think to say.

Alex helped him into the back seat, admonishing him to watch his head. He was purposely kind to him. In the next few hours there would be much the two of them would discuss, and he didn't necessarily want to start off on too much of an adversarial foot—not until he had to.

Primes asked, "Are you arresting the others too?"

"Nope, just you for now."

"Why me? I don't understand."

"You will. Now, I'd appreciate it if you sit back there and keep your mouth shut until we get to the station."

"I'm going to be booked?"

"Yes. Now, please be quiet!"

Gerald Primes tried to sit back to get as comfortable as possible, with hands cuffed behind his back, shoulder blades screaming for mercy in what now felt like a very tight suit jacket, there wasn't much comfort to be found. What will I tell my wife? he wondered. Attempted murder? Who—that writer woman? And, which of the meetings with Lyle and Frank had they taped? Gerald couldn't quite figure it out, but he knew he was in serious trouble.

At approximately twelve-thirty they arrived at FBI head-quarters. Gerald fought panic. The FBI! This was worse than he thought.

"When you flashed your badge I didn't realize you were with the FBI."

"You know it now," Alex replied, gripping his upper arm and leading him down the hall. "We'll talk in here."

He pulled out a chair and coaxed Gerald into it. Alex thought about removing the cuffs, but a little discomfort for a while longer might be a good thing.

"I'm Alex Powers, and I will primarily be responsible for taking your statement."

"What statement? I don't have anything to say."

"Hmmm, that's interesting. You had plenty to say the night of December 1st with your buddies, Lyle and Frank."

"I have no idea what you're talking about."

"Okay, let me ask you something. Are you in any way associated with a Dr. Zimmerman of Comex Manufacturing?"

"No," Gerald stated matter-of-factly.

"Are you aware of or have any knowledge about a conspiracy to disfigure people of color?"

Gerald hesitated for a moment. "No."

"Are you aware of an incident of breaking and entering, destroying property, and killing an animal at one of your co-worker's home?"

His mind reeling, Gerald didn't answer the question. How much does he know? he wondered.

"I'm waiting for your answer."

"Can you take these things off my wrists? They're killing me!"

"No. Since you seem to have a very short memory, let me help you a bit."

Alex tapped the two-way glass window twice, and an agent appeared with a tape recorder. Alex pressed play, and watched with satisfaction the horrified look that crossed Gerald's face when he heard his own voice. Alex stopped the tape at the part where the discussion began about killing Danithia's dog.

"How's your memory now, Mr. Primes?"

Gerald began to sweat. It dripped in his eyes, and he tried to wipe it away, shrugging his shoulders, but with each movement the cuffs bit deeper into his wrists, causing him to sweat even more.

"Please, can you take the cuffs off?"

"Perhaps. And I could even get you something to drink, but first we need to establish some ground rules, okay?"

"What ground rules?"

"First, when I ask you a question, you answer it promptly and truthfully. Second, and this is important, depending upon how helpful you are to me, I just might get you out of this mess. Understand?"

"Yes," Gerald said tartly. "I am a lawyer, after all."

"Great." Again, Alex tapped on the glass, and immediately another officer appeared and placed a soft drink in front of Gerald, then released him from the metal bracelets.

Alex said, "Let me just tell you that I have enough evidence to send you and your partners to prison for a very long time. But I get the feeling that this wasn't really your idea, that somehow you got coerced into becoming involved. Am I right?"

"Yes." Gerald nodded emphatically. "Yes, I got talked into it."

"I see. And you had no idea what you were getting involved in, did you?"

"No. No sir, I sure didn't."

"So who was the mastermind?"

Gerald did not answer.

Without compunction, Alex kicked the chair out from under him and Gerald landed with a heavy thud.

"Hey! Why'd you do that?"

"'Cause I told you the rules, and I'm not into repeating myself. Now, you agreed to answer my questions promptly and truthfully, did you not!" Alex shouted, his voice echoing off the walls in this tiny room.

"Yes. Yes."

"All right now, don't make me have to kick your behind in here. Answer my question."

"I want a lawyer. I'm not answering any more questions."

"So now we're going to play this game. Okay." Alex righted the chair and Gerald gingerly sat. "Which lawyer would you like me to call? Lyle or Frank? I'd venture to say, once Lyle gets here, and he's led to believe that you squealed, he'll turn on you quick as lightning. And then, once I get Frank in here, oh I'm sure he'll be more than

willing to rat your little scrawny ass out faster than I can say
his one-syllable last name."

Alex, perched on the edge of the table, got up and
headed for the door. He tapped three times, and an officer
entered with a cordless telephone. He placed it with great
care right beside Gerald's hand, then retreated.

Alex stood in the corner and watched him. He didn't
utter another word for several minutes, just watched
Gerald fight with himself.

"Go ahead, Gerald, call your lawyer. But let me just
warn you that, as soon as you pick up that phone, I'm
going to tap on this glass again and this time, as swiftly as
everything else has happened thus far, an order for a grand
jury to convene will be prepared, and—" Alex approached
Gerald and sat on the nearest chair. "You can rest assured
that indictments will be handed up for you and your partners." He paused. "It's your choice."

Gerald quivered in his seat. He did not know what to
do. "What happens if I don't call an attorney? What happens if I talk to you?"

"Then, depending upon what you tell us, we might cut
you a deal in return for your sworn testimony against Lyle
McGregor, Franklin Ditz, Dr. Zimmerman, and anybody
else you can connect to the case."

"Total immunity?"

Alex drummed his fingers on the table. After a
moment, he removed a fresh tape from his pocket and
snapped it into the recorder.

Then he smiled. "Tell me what you know."

~ ~ ~

"Look," Gerald began, "you have to understand that I had
little to do with any of this."

"I'll make that determination. Let's get to the story."

"Okay." Gerald paused, wiped a sweaty palm against his forehead, took a deep breath, and began.

"After the civil rights movement and the assassination of Dr. King, it seemed that Blacks were taking over every- thing. They were in our schools, sitting wherever they wanted in restaurants, there just didn't seem to be anyplace they weren't penetrating our White infra-structure. That was bad enough, but then when Blacks started infiltrating politics, well, then we realized we had to draw the line."

"Who's 'we'?" Alex asked.

"Those of us who liked having the world—the United States— in our control. Look, we're not monsters—really— " he stammered, looked at the floor, and nervously back again at Alex. "Not monsters at all."

"That's your personal opinion. I beg to differ. Are we talking White supremacists?"

"We hate that title. It's so..." He waved his hands. "It's not accurate enough. But—okay, yes."

"Go on." Alex prompted.

"We had the backing of some very powerful people."

"Who?"

Gerald grinned. "Oh, Mr. high-and-mighty FBI agent, you'd be surprised."

"And I guess you've forgotten who you're dealing with. It would be no sweat off my brow to commence to whip- ping your scrawny little weasel ass right now. I suggest you keep your smart comments out of this before I forget who I work for."

Nervously twitching in his chair, Gerald watched Alex's feet, as if he feared to have the chair once more kicked from underneath him.

"Now," Alex continued. "I asked you a question, and I told you before that I am not inclined to repeat myself. So!" he shouted, "who are we talking about?"

"The government, okay? The United States government backs us, financially and otherwise. We are completely supported by your employer," Gerald said and began to laugh hysterically.

Alex watched him for a time, not sure if he should believe his ears. He had stumbled upon something much bigger than he could ever have imagined. He made a quick decision and turned the recorder off, walked over to the two-way mirror and pulled the curtain. Then he flipped a switch which silenced their voices. Nobody could hear or see them now, and the door was locked from the inside.

In a menacing whisper, he asked him, "Why?"

"Why?" Gerald croaked. "Why? Because this is our country and we want it back!"

"So you're trying to make me believe that the United States government—my employer as you so eloquently reminded me—is behind this conspiracy. Is that what you're trying to tell me?"

"I'm not trying. I am telling you."

"And my government is behind disfiguring Black people?"

"Powerful, influential Blacks, not just anybody."

"How many?"

"How many what?"

"First, I want to know how many victims."

"I don't know."

Alex gave him a fierce look. "You don't know?"

"No, I don't know."

"I don't believe that. But, let's say it's true, and you don't know. Can you find out?"

He stammered and stuttered, "I—don't know. They don't let me in on too much."

"Probably because you're a coward. Okay, for now I'll leave that alone. What governmental agency funds this little conspiracy?"

"I don't know."

"You don't know!" Alex screamed at him, spittle showering Gerald's face. "I tell you what. You better give me a name, or I will not be responsible for what happens to you next!"

"Look mister, beating me to a bloody pulp isn't going to get you what you want. It's really very simple. If I say I don't know, I really don't know."

Alex watched him for a time. How true were the things Gerald said? What information could he get from this worthless piece of shit? He knew from listening to his voice on the tape that he was a wimp, but he'd hoped Primes would at least have the information he needed to solve this case and move on.

Gerald said, a whining, pleading note in his voice, "All I can tell you is, it's not a known governmental agency. It's covert or something."

Alex looked at him with a puzzled frown. "What did you say ... covert?"

"Yeah, yeah, you know, undercover."

Alex narrowed his eyes. "The organization isn't called 'covert'?"

"How should I know? I told you they don't let me in on a whole lot."

"Hmm. Be quiet and let me think for a minute!"

Alex paced the room. Was it his own organization "COVERT" that was behind these atrocities? How could that be? He was always on assignments where they dismantled these type of organizations? Was it all a scam? Had he been chasing his own tail and not known it? Was he unknowingly a participant in the evil acts perpetrated against Danithia? Had they both somehow stumbled too close to the truth?

"This is what I want you to do." He grabbed a pencil and paper and shoved it at Gerald. "Write down everything you know and I do mean everything! Do not leave out a single detail! When you're finished I'm going to take you someplace safe. You'll have to lie low until I can check into some things."

"Hey, I can't just disappear. I'm in the middle of preparing for a trial."

"Tough! You obviously don't understand the danger you're in, do you, stupid?"

Gerald flinched.

Alex watched this pitiful little man and suddenly felt sorry for him.

"Look, I apologize. There's no need for me to call you names. I need to protect you. Understand that what I'm about to do is in your best interest."

"How am I supposed to handle not going to work? And . . . what about my wife!"

"Call in sick, have a relative die or in the hospital. I don't care, just make something up."

Neither Alex nor Gerald knew that at that moment they were making a pact that would turn into a friendship that would last for several weeks.

Chapter 15

Alex paced the floor in his modest-sized office. He wondered what and how much to tell Danithia. And he wondered if she'd be angry or mad at him once he told her what he'd been doing the past several weeks. Although he had wanted to tell her ever since that night he'd grabbed Gerald Primes and interrogated him, somehow the time never seemed right.

He heard the front door open and softly close. Taking a deep breath, he headed for the living room. "Hey, babe."

"Hey yourself," she replied, a bit weary.

"How did it go today?"

"Okay, just tiresome. I spent a great deal of the day trying to decide how to handle my meeting with Comex tomorrow."

"Good, good," he said, his voice trailing off. He stroked his jaw, feeling the rough, prickly texture, and realized he really needed to shave.

"Alex, honey, what's the matter?"

"Babe, I'm not sure you're going to like what I've got to say."

Danithia watched his brow furrow in obvious discomfort, and her heart sank. "What's this about, Alex? You're scaring me."

"Babe, indictments are coming down by the end of the week for Lyle and Franklin, for their participation in the conspiracy with Comex."

Danithia stared at him for a long time, then she plopped heavily down on the sofa.

"I don't understand. I thought you told me they were small fish in a big pond and that your organization wasn't really looking at them. When did that change?"

"The night I arrested Gerald."

She gasped. "You arrested Gerald? Gerald Primes?" she almost shouted.

"Yes. He was the weak link in the chain, so my superiors and I decided to grab him—see what information we could get from him."

"Weak link? What are you talking about?"

"Babe, all the things that happened to you—the tire slashing, the break-in, the loss of the dog—it was all because you and I were getting too close to the truth about Comex. The tape we were supposed to look at—the one that was stolen—it held a viable piece of evidence."

She sat very still and said nothing.

"Babe, I had a wire—a hidden tape recorder—in almost all the offices at your firm."

She looked at him, and her eyes narrowed. "Even my office, Alex?"

"Yes." He looked away. "Even yours."

"This is incredible. I can't believe my own husband tapped me. What were you looking for? What did you expect to hear?"

"Evidence. Evidence of the crimes we were both concerned about. Danithia, please believe me, it was never done for the purpose of spying on you."

She continued to stare at him, not sure what to believe.

"Go on with your story, Alex," she said in a cold voice.

"Babe, what happened? Did you forget what I do? Spying is part of how I find out what criminals are doing."

"But me, Alex?" she queried. "I was considered a criminal, too?"

Exasperated, he ran a hand through his hair. "Danithia, I had to bug the entire office, okay. Don't you want to know what I found out?"

She said nothing.

He knelt on the floor in front of her and took her hands in his, almost the same way as on the night he'd asked her to marry him.

"Lyle, Franklin, and Gerald, were all part of this enormous plan to systematically eliminate any and all threats to their false impression that White people should rule the world."

She still did not speak but sat very still, her gaze on their joined hands.

His heart sank. "Babe, remember all those nights when I was up late and you had already gone to bed?"

He waited, but she did not answer him, nor did she look him in the eye.

"During those times, I was listening to surveillance tapes. One night I heard everything I needed to hear to put them away." He watched her solemn face. Taking a deep breath, he began again. "If it'll make you feel any better, I never listened to the goings-on in your office. Somebody else did that. Remember, I was busy during the day pretending to be a security officer. I didn't have time to listen to tapes then."

"Oh," she almost shouted. "Am I supposed to be happy that you didn't eavesdrop on me, but somebody else did!"

"No," he said, frustrated. "Babe, I'm only saying that I never spied on you, only on your co-workers."

Alex's knees became numb. He winced when he stood, then sat beside her. He began to gently massage her belly.

"Babe, do you doubt my love for you?"

She said nothing, but he saw a lonesome tear roll down her cheek. It landed on his hand. He lifted her chin and stared into her eyes—eyes he thought were the most beautiful in the world, even when they were shrouded with pain. He watched her chin tremble. Her nose turned red as even more tears cascaded down her cheeks.

"I feel so violated," she whispered.

"No babe, no. It was never intended that way, not for you. It was a further way to protect you. Remember that for a while you were a target? I couldn't risk anything more happening to you. I couldn't be with you twenty-four seven, so I had them tap your office. I mean, what if someone had threatened you? I wouldn't know, and we'd need proof. Think about it, babe. Please, don't you see that what happened had to happen the way it happened."

"No," she said coldly. "I don't see it that way at all. What I see is a husband that betrayed me. A husband who should have told me exactly what he was doing."

"I couldn't, Danithia."

She placed her hand atop his and removed it from her belly. "I want to be alone for a while, Alex. Just leave me alone."

He watched her walk away, her head down, and he knew—he felt her disappointment.

She entered the bathroom, her sanctuary, and started her bath water. The fragrant scent of magnolias filled the air. Even though she loved this scent, it did not calm her troubled spirit. She gingerly lowered herself into the warm water and waited for her belly to dance. The first time she felt the first flutterings of life she was in the bathtub. Now, it was somewhat of a ritual for her to watch with fascination, as her baby would come to life, stretching and kicking when she was engulfed in water. She sat very still and waited. Nothing happened.

"Come on, little one," she coaxed. "Are you sleeping?" She gently caressed her belly, stroking it from side to side. At one point, she even shook her tummy, trying to awaken the sleeping baby inside. There were no stirrings at all, not even a flutter. She felt the beginning of panic starting to rise deep within her, but she would not allow herself to get even more upset than she already was. Alex's revelations were disconcerting enough.

When she got into bed, Alex was already there, watching her, an expectant expression upon his face.

"Are you still angry with me?" he asked.

"Alex, I'm tired. I don't want to talk about this anymore tonight."

~ ~ ~

Spring had come and gone, and a beautiful summer was beginning. Danithia awoke, stretched and yawned. She examined her naked body in the mirror and was surprised at how much her belly had expanded and stretched to proportions she never would have thought possible. Until now.

It was becoming the norm for her to have back pain, or her ankles swelled, making her look even more like an overinflated balloon than before. She missed her feet—missed them more than she thought she ever would. It was amazing what things, you suddenly realize, you've always taken for granted. Like putting on shoes or lacing up sneakers, and doing so without gasping for air or trying to figure out a way to get around an ample belly to complete the task. It seemed she was always calling Alex's name to button this, or tie that, or she found herself asking that age-old question, "Am I fat?" knowing full-well the answer.

And Alex, dear sweet Alex, always answered her in the affirmative, telling her with a smile that, yes, she was fat, and then reminded her that she was also happy and carry-

ing in her womb a healthy, chubby baby. Then he promised her that he would exercise with her after the baby was
born, that he'd run with her and even, if she wanted it,
design an exercise room for her once the baby arrived. He
ended each statement with a promise to love her forever—
big or small—skinny or fat, he loved her unconditionally.

She watched him sleep and tears filled her eyes. How
many times had she acted stupid and childish, but Alex
never judged her. But was she overreacting to what he'd
told her last night? Could she continue to live with a man
who she wasn't sure she could trust anymore? Soon she
would have a little girl or boy to shower her love upon,
would Alex still be in the picture to do the same? She did-
n't know and that frightened her.

~ ~ ~

Today, she was attending a meeting with the attorneys for
Comex, presumably to talk again about the possibility of
settlement. She dressed carefully, concerned that her pregnancy might make her appear fragile or unable to fight.
That was the farthest thing from the truth. It amazed her
that men could imagine a woman who possessed a lot of
fire before her pregnancy would suddenly have none as
maternal instincts took over. Wrong! Danithia was more
than ready to fight. And, she thought, she'd be even more
ready if her backache would go away. It would be difficult
to appear like someone to be reckoned with if her face was
contorted with pain.

"Alex!" she called. "Please help me zip this dress.
Damn, dress! Who designed this thing? I mean who
would put a zipper on the back of a maternity dress?"

"I've been watching you for a while. I wondered when,
and if, you'd ask me to help. You must still be angry with
me."

She said nothing, just turned her back to him so he could zip the dress.

He finished the task, then risked cradling her in his arms, hoping she wouldn't pull away. He loved holding her this way. With her back against him and his arms surrounding and cradling her belly, he could sometimes feel the baby move or kick. Often he was disappointed when his son or daughter didn't react to his touch, like now. But the feeling that he was protecting both of them at the same time when he held her this way was the main reason he enjoyed it. A profound sense of joy came over him when she relaxed against his body and leaned the back of her head against his chest. He felt her take a deep breath and let it out slowly, as if she were pushing all bad thoughts, feelings, and ideas away.

He kissed the side of her head and stroked her tummy. "I love you."

~ ~ ~

Once Danithia arrived at the office of Comex, she felt a certain energy that at first was not readily identifiable. She was ushered into an elaborately decorated conference room with an enormous oval-shaped table capable of comfortably seating thirty people. She chose to seat herself at the head of the table, facing a picturesque view of the Colorado mountains. Immediately, she pulled documentation that outlined her client's demands from her briefcase. Her list was divided into two categories: one column indicated negotiable items, and the other noted items that were not, under any circumstances, negotiable.

"Good morning, Ms. Gilberts."

"Mr. Ivy." she replied and nodded.

He approached her, extending his hand. "It's so nice to see you again."

"Thank you. I wish I could say the same. The last time we met was anything but pleasant, if you recall."

"Yes, yes. I remember. Please have a seat. Let's talk."

Danithia eyed him suspiciously. His manner was not at all confrontational as she had expected.

"I'd like to apologize for the way our first meeting went. I have to admit that I was a bit over-zealous that day and may have mis-spoken."

"Mis-spoken?"

"Yes, yes. Regarding Comex's position on this particular litigation."

"And just what is Comex's position today, Mr. Ivy?"

"We are prepared to meet all of your client's demands, within reason, of course, in order to come to an amicable settlement for both parties today."

Danithia observed his mannerisms, noting the way he seemed to be seated uncomfortably, his hands never at rest, his eyes often darting about the room.

"Mr. Ivy, you don't even know what my client's demands are. How can you possibly agree to meet all of them today?"

"If you'll recall, I said 'within reason,' and I'm sure you and your client are reasonable people."

"We are indeed reasonable people, but this was an unreasonable and senseless crime, and it won't be dealt with as if it were anything but that."

"Agreed," he stammered. "Agreed."

"My client will settle for forty million dollars per each known and unknown plaintiff, up to a total of fifty people."

"Make it thirty people, and you've got a deal."

Danithia glanced at her notes and smiled. She and Patricia had agreed on twenty-five, but he didn't have to know that.

"Okay, thirty."

Mr. Ivy fidgeted with his tie and brushed back a few wayward strands of hair. "Good, good."

"Not so fast, Mr. Ivy. We also want Comex to put funding toward research to undo the physical damage sustained by my clients."

"We're already on it. Anything else?"

"Yes. My clients are demanding that a significant amount of funding go toward education."

"Education?"

"Yes, education. We feel that if youngsters are taught tolerance and respect for one another and the differences in our respective cultures, then perhaps we can prevent this type of heinous crime from happening again."

"How much funding?"

"A significant amount. We'll have to do the research to figure out exactly how much will be required to start a program at the elementary school level."

"I'll have to get back to my superiors about that one."

"Mr. Ivy, this is not negotiable."

He squirmed in his seat, choosing to stare out the window.

"Also," Danithia said. "My clients want a public admission of liability and guilt."

He jumped up, startling Danithia.

"No!" he shouted. "No admission of guilt and, furthermore, no disclosure of this settlement will ever go public. And that—" He paused. "That is not negotiable, Ms. Gilberts."

"Mr. Ivy, please, there is no need to shout. I can hear you just fine."

Danithia looked down at her notes. Admission of liability was in the negotiable column. She had fought long and hard with Patricia about this one. Danithia knew that Comex would never, ever publicly admit liability. An admission of guilt would mean certain disaster for this pub-licly-held corporation.

At last, Mr. Ivy spoke again, more quietly now. "I apol-ogize, but understand that the terms of our settlement will be completely under seal."

"Agreed," Danithia said. "Oh, and one more thing, Mr. Ivy."

He sighed and seemed to brace himself.

"Ms. Griffin will be leaving for Europe soon, and I want her entire trip paid for outside of the settlement. I want an all-expenses-paid trip for her, from where she chooses to stay, her treatments there, right down to what she elects to eat each day, that entire trip will be compliments of Comex."

He eyed her for a moment, looked as if he was about to protest, then said. "Done."

Danithia smiled. "I'll expect a draft settlement agree-ment within the next few days."

She stood and began placing paperwork back in her briefcase. The last item she had asked for wasn't even on her list, she just thought that, because Comex was being so generous, the least they could do was pay for this trip. Patricia had lost income ever since this whole thing hap-pened, and it had stifled her ability to write. Danithia believed Comex should somehow pay for that too, so an all-expense-paid trip to Europe would have to do.

~ ~ ~

After such a long, but successful day, Danithia returned home to find that Alex had cleaned and cooked. The house smelled wonderful. She peeked inside one of the pots to see that he had roasted a chicken, and prepared vegetables, garlic bread was baking in the oven. Alex was not there.

She headed toward the bedroom, but stopped short when she saw him in the bathroom, sitting atop the toilet seat, a bouquet of red roses in his hand and her bath water running. The strong scent of peaches permeated the air and she smiled. "Hi."

"Did you have a good day?"

"Wonderful. Patricia got almost everything she wanted, including a trip to Europe that they'll pay for. She was so pleased when I called to tell her."

She could tell that he was only half listening to her, that his attention was on whether or not she had forgiven him. "Are those flowers for me?"

He smiled, extending them to her. "Yes."

"Why do men always think that flowers gets them out of the doghouse?"

"'Cause sometimes it does. Did it work for me this time?"

She didn't answer him, she just took the flowers from him, sat them on the counter top, and began to undress. She stepped into the bathtub and sat down with a sigh.

"I'm sorry I couldn't tell you, babe," Alex said.

"Me too. It feels strange to know that someone was listening to everything I did or said for the last several months. But, at least, what you heard will result in indictments? But aren't taps inadmissible evidence? I may not practice criminal law, but I do know the basics."

"The taps were just a stepping stone we used to get to a real source of information. That source turned out to be Gerald."

"Yes and here we all thought Gerald's father was ill, and he was visiting him somewhere on the East Coast."

"That's the story we concocted. By the time we got through with Gerald, we had enough concrete evidence to indict Lyle and Franklin and a whole bunch of other people, even members of my organization, COVERT."

She looked at him with shock, splashed water onto the floor when she suddenly sat up. "Your organization too?"

"It's such a long story. I wanted to tell you all about it last night, but, well . . ."

"I didn't want to hear it last night. Tell me everything now."

He looked at her grateful to hear the concern and love she had for him return to her voice. "There were certain members of COVERT who were also advocates of White supremacy. The surveillance tape had one of my agents on it."

She gasped. "Really!"

"And he wasn't the only one. It's ironic, that the very thing the agents were employed to help stop was really something they wanted to see happen." He shook his head when he remembered how these men were discovered— men he'd worked with, had a drink with, and put his life on the line with. What was even more shocking was that they had a long-range plan to eliminate Alex, too. He wouldn't tell Danithia about that though.

She asked, "Are the indictments why Comex settled so easily today?"

"I don't know. I really can't say. Comex is guilty too, but mainly their guilt stems from not handling their business with Dr. Zimmerman. They gave that man too much freedom. They didn't watch him, so now they have to pay."

They sat quietly for a minute. There was much more Alex wanted to tell her, but he was finally back on solid ground with her, he didn't want to blow it now.

"The baby hasn't been moving much lately," she said her brow wrinkling, as she cradled her belly and gently shook it.

"Really," Alex said alarmed. "Since when?"

"Yesterday. That's when I first noticed it."

"Okay," Alex said fighting the urge to panic. "Think about your day. Did the baby kick and move around while you were at your office, or at your meeting with Comex?"

She still cradled her belly, then stroked it, while she thought about it.

"I honestly don't remember feeling her kick. Alex," she said alarmed. "Do you think the baby's okay?"

"I don't know babe. Just try to stay calm. Why don't you get out of the tub so we can go to the hospital or something," he said his voice trembling.

This could not be happening to him again. He thought he could not bear the loss of another child. He placed his hand atop her abdomen and stroked her. He splashed water on her belly and waited. His eyes were closed as he concentrated, willing the baby to move.

"See what I mean," Danithia wailed. "You know how much this baby likes being in water. And now, no activity at all!" she shrieked.

"It's okay, babe," he said as he continued to stroke and caress her.

With a sudden force that surprised him, Danithia's belly expanded and a series of quick sharp blows pounded the palm of his hand.

They both stared at each other.

"She's okay," he murmured.

"Wow," Danithia exclaimed. "That was hard. I guess she wanted us to know she's fine."

Alex brushed back tears of joy. He had never been so scared in all his life. He couldn't speak. Then, the baby kicked again, as hard as before.

"She wants your hand off her behind now," Danithia said, teasing.

"No, it's my boy. He wants to show me how hard he can kick."

She groaned. "Whoever's in there, they need to stop kicking me so hard." She cradled her belly. "Okay, I know you're all right in there little one, stop kicking mommy so hard."

They stared at each other for a long time. "I love you, Danithia. With all my heart I love you."

"We love you too," she said and put his hand atop her stomach again.

"Alex, do you feel like washing my hair?"

"Anything you want, babe, anything at all."

Danithia loved having Alex wash her hair. He massaged her scalp and the feel of his strong hands manipulating and circling her scalp made her feel totally relaxed. This was a sensual dance between the two of them that would make her nipples hard, and she always had an incredible urge to make love afterward.

As she closed her eyes and enjoyed this moment, in her mind, they were closing the door on the past and re-entering the life they were used to. No more Comex. Just the two—no, three of them. Now, everything would be as it should be, back to normal.

Vicki Andrews lives in San Diego. She is a performance poet, lecturer, novelist, and short story writer. Currently she is the Vice President of the African American Writers & Artists, Inc. of San Diego.

INDIGO: Sensuous Love Stories *Order Form*

Mail to:
Genesis Press, Inc.
315 3rd Avenue North
Columbus, MS 39701

Visit our website at

http://www.genesis-press.com

Name——————————————

Address——————————————

City/State/Zip——————————————

1999 INDIGO TITLES

Qty	Title	Author	Price	Total
	Somebody's Someone	Sinclair LeBeau	$8.95	
	Interlude	Donna Hill	$8.95	
	The Price of Love	Beverly Clark	$8.95	
	Unconditional Love	Alicia Wiggins	$8.95	
	Mae's Promise	Melody Walcott	$8.95	
	Whispers in the Night	Dorothy Love	$8.95	
	No Regrets (paperback reprint)	Mildred Riley	$8.95	
	Kiss or Keep	D.Y. Phillips	$8.95	
	Naked Soul (paperback reprint)	Gwynne Forster	$8.95	
	Pride and Joi (paperback Reprint)	Gay G. Gunn	$8.95	
	A Love to Cherish (paperback reprint)	Beverly Clark	$8.95	
	Caught in a Trap	Andree Jackson	$8.95	
	Truly Inseparable (paperback reprint)	Wanda Thomas	$8.95	
	A Lighter Shade of Brown	Vicki Andrews	$8.95	
	Cajun Heat	Charlene Berry	$8.95	

Use this order form
or call:

1-888-INDIGO1

(1-888-463-4461)

TOTAL _____

Shipping & Handling _____

($3.00 first book $1.00 each additional book)

TOTAL Amount Enclosed _____

MS Residents add 7% sales tax